"Don't be so shy."

Jill patted her lap. The guy was really good-looking, she noted as he awkwardly lowered himself to sit. And he had a great tush. But Santa wasn't supposed to notice things like that. Especially when she had two of Maury's goons hot on her trail.

"So, little boy. What do you want for Christmas?" she asked in her gruff Santa voice, sliding an arm around his waist.

"Watch it, buddy," the man warned.

Jill couldn't believe the guy didn't realize she was a woman. "I don't think I've heard of that toy. Is there another one you want?"

He was clearly not amused. "How about a stun gun?"

Jill smiled. Maybe hiding out in a Santa suit wasn't such a bad idea after all. "Santa doesn't believe in guns. How about a blow-up doll?"

The man stood up in disbelief, fixing her with an incredulous gaze.

He was really cute when he was dumbstruck, Jill thought. "Well, you can let me know next time you're in the mall. And by the way," she couldn't help adding, *"nice buns."*

Dear Reader,

Ho, ho, ho! 'Tis the season for jolly St. Nick, chestnuts roasting over an open fire and mistletoe carefully hung in *strategic* doorways (kissing, after all, is a very serious matter). It's also a great season for LOVE & LAUGHTER. We're celebrating with two wonderfully funny, always entertaining and very romantic holiday books.

Temptation favorite Alyssa Dean spins a tale of mischief, family and the true meaning of Christmas in *Mistletoe Mischief*. As Josh professes frequently, he doesn't mind the yuletide season, he just doesn't have time for it! I think you'll be just as delighted with Josh Larkland's Christmas turnaround as he is!

Debbi Rawlins writes about a different type of Santa, a Santa undercover. Santa is really Jill Tanner, a woman on the run for her life who ends up hiding out in the last place she would expect—a suburban home that's missing a very crucial element, a mother. Try getting out of that conundrum and baking Christmas cookies at the same time! Debbi continues to delight her fans with stories for Harlequin American Romance.

Wishing you all the joys of the holiday season (and lots of good presents!),

Malle Vallik

Malle Vallik
Associate Senior Editor

I SAW DADDY KISSING SANTA CLAUS

Debbi Rawlins

Harlequin Books

TORONTO • NEW YORK • LONDON
AMSTERDAM • PARIS • SYDNEY • HAMBURG
STOCKHOLM • ATHENS • TOKYO • MILAN
MADRID • WARSAW • BUDAPEST • AUCKLAND

ISBN 0-373-44034-0

I SAW DADDY KISSING SANTA CLAUS

Copyright © 1997 by Debbi Quattrone

A funny thing happened...

I love Christmas and all its pageantry. Even the stress of shopping, decorating and cooking excites me. My only stresser is the annual battle of the bulge, trying to squeeze into party dresses that got impossibly smaller in one short year. But you know, this year I might just take Jill's lead. When I eat too many cookies, I'll just skip the party dress and go right for the Santa suit. I only hope I need *some* padding....

—Debbi Rawlins

Books by Debbi Rawlins

HARLEQUIN AMERICAN ROMANCE
580—MARRIAGE INCORPORATED
618—THE COWBOY AND THE CENTERFOLD
622—THE OUTLAW AND THE CITY SLICKER
675—LOVE, MARRIAGE AND OTHER CALAMITIES
691—MARRY ME, BABY

This is for Brenda Chin, American Airlines and the Dallas airport. Sometimes a delayed flight really pays off.

1

JILL MORGAN HAD A BIRD'S-EYE VIEW of Maury's two henchmen, until Santa Claus took a spill and landed in a sorry heap of red velvet and fake white fur at her feet. Worse, the commotion drew the attention of nearby shoppers in the department store.

Cringing as several pairs of eyes stared at the stockroom where she hid, Jill dived for cover under the heavily flocked branches of an artificial Christmas tree. She landed uncomfortably close to Santa, and sucked in a breath. The sharp tang of cheap scotch stung her nostrils.

Wrinkling her nose in disbelief, she stared at the man. Santa was stinking drunk.

What in Sam Hill was going on today? It had to be a full moon or something. Her luck was catapulting from bad to worse. Of course if she didn't get out of this stockroom...out of this store...out of this mall without being spotted, all the luck in the world wasn't going to save her butt.

Scrambling into a crouched position, she hunkered low enough to stay hidden by the partially assembled tree, then scanned the faces of several anxious shoppers peering in through the open stockroom door. Old Saint Nick continued to lie spread-eagle on the floor, like a big red attention magnet. A hellacious snore erupted from his bulbous nose, sending a shudder through his long white beard.

That did it. Jill had to do something. Poking her head up

a few inches, she saw Maury's goons searching the toy aisle. Any minute, they'd be closing in on the stockroom.

She muttered darkly under her breath and stared at the little girl with long honey-colored braids who stood at the threshold and continued to gape at Santa. She definitely had to get rid of the kid. Or better yet...

Jill looked past the girl to make sure Maury's thugs weren't nearby. Seeing that the aisle was clear, she ducked out a tad and whispered, "Hey, little girl, close the door, would you?"

Santa cut loose another rip-roaring snore, and the child jumped, her attention glued to the red heap.

Great. Keeping an eye out the door, Jill sank back on her haunches while "Jingle Bells" played for at least the tenth time since she'd been hiding in the store. She had to get out of here before Maury's search party found her and dragged her back to the wedding. Christmas was only a week away. If she could disappear until New Year's Day, she'd be safe for another year. After all, Maury was more interested in his tax status than in actually putting a ring on her finger.

Jill edged forward once more.

"Look, sweetie, he's just taking a short nap," she said in a hushed voice, although she doubted the kid would buy that explanation. No more than Jill would have at age five or six. By then, Jill had already experienced too many disappointments. At six she'd known Santa and Prince Charming were both lies. "Now, be a good girl and close the door."

The child stood frozen.

Sighing, Jill eyed the distance between them, her palms growing moist. She had about ten seconds to decide what to do. Goon number one was nowhere in sight. Number two stood at the far end of the aisle ogling the chocolate reindeers.

She inched away from the tree, her pulse leaping when she bumped into a semiclothed mannequin. This was crazy. What could they do to her in a crowded mall, anyway? Except these guys weren't the typical idiots who hung around her employer. They looked mean. And worse…stupid. She took another look at the one with the sweet tooth. Maybe she was just being paranoid, but below Sweet Tooth's short fat neck, below his linebacker shoulders, his navy jacket bulged where it shouldn't.

She shivered. Maybe the rumors about Maury were true.

Nah, he wouldn't hurt her, she thought, staring warily out into the store. Would he?

Out of choices, long out of luck, Jill made a quick grab for the door. Surprised, the little girl stumbled out of the way, and Jill said, ''Sorry, kid,'' right before she pulled the door shut.

After promptly securing the lock, she dragged a broken sleigh across for good measure. Then she turned with disgust toward the man with the crooked white beard.

''I could've made a run for it if you hadn't kicked up such a racket, you turkey,'' she said, glaring at him. ''Hey, wake up.''

Jill shook his shoulder, knowing it wouldn't do any good. She had too much experience with drunks. When he didn't budge, she yanked the fake beard, letting it snap back into place.

The man coughed and sputtered, sending up a cloud of stale scotch that pinched the air from her lungs. Rearing her head back, Jill coughed and sputtered. Santa sank deeper into oblivion.

''You're a disgrace to the uniform, buddy. You don't

have any business wearing it. A bunch of disappointed kids are probably waiting, and you..."

She blinked, an inspiration forming. Was she crazy? This was perfect.

A slow grin lifted the corners of her mouth as she started to hum a lullaby. She didn't know the words, but he snored louder so it was obviously doing the trick.

She smiled, unbuckled his belt, then pulled off his clunky battered boots. Positioning herself at his stocking feet, she quickly grabbed the white-fur cuffs of his pants.

"Mister, I sure hope you have on underwear," she said, and taking a deep breath, she gave a firm tug.

NOAH SPENSER hated malls. He wasn't fond of standing in line, either. But his seven-year-old daughter, Mindy, wanted to sit on Santa's lap and there was no way in hell he would disappoint her. Especially not after the rough year she'd just had.

"Daddy?" Mindy tugged at his hand, her bright green eyes widening as they followed the train circling the display-window Christmas tree. "What time is Santa supposed to come?"

Spenser glanced at his watch. "He should be here any minute, honey. Do you want an ice-cream cone while we wait?"

"But then we'd have to get out of line." Her attention stayed glued to the train, then her gaze abruptly darted to the ice-cream parlor three stores down before settling on his face. "Or I could get it while you wait here."

He shifted positions and smiled. She tested him like this from time to time. As if she knew that he was uneasy about what to do or say, or whether he was too smothering. Although he'd always taken an active role in parenting, since her mother left a little over a year ago, Mindy was his full-time project.

"Well…" He rubbed his jaw, then let his fingers trail to the back of his neck. He needed a haircut…he needed some sleep…he needed Ann Landers. "Uh, maybe, uh, hey, there's Santa now."

He scooped Mindy up so that she could see over everyone's heads. She squirmed to get into an advantageous position and he caught a whiff of baby powder. He had no idea if she was too old for that sort of thing, but he dusted her tummy daily because the scent reminded him of when she was a baby, of happier times. Before her mother left them.

All the kids started to murmur above the Christmas carols playing over the mall sound system, and the crowd pressed against them as Santa got closer. Spenser held their third-place-in-line position as he absently watched Santa approach his throne.

Keeping track of the man wasn't easy. Spenser frowned, wondering why the mall had hired such a scrawny Santa. The man couldn't have been more than five-five, and even with all his padding, it was obvious he was of slight build. Spenser's frown deepened. The guy sure had a funny walk.

"Daddy? Do you want to know what I'm gonna ask Santa for?"

"Sure," he said softly.

"I want another Cabbage Patch doll, maybe a Barbie doll, a playhouse…" She pursed her lips, her dark eyebrows pulling together. "How many things do you think he'll bring me?"

Spenser smiled, grateful she'd excluded the one wish Santa couldn't deliver. "As much as he can fit in his bag, I guess."

Mindy grinned back and eyed the large white sack

stuffed with colorfully wrapped packages sitting beside the throne. Santa finally settled in to arrange his lopsided stomach, and Spenser shook his head. Surely mall management could have done better than this.

"Why isn't Santa saying ho-ho-ho?" Mindy asked as Spenser set her back down on the floor.

Obviously having heard her, the boy in front of them yelled out, "Ho-ho-ho."

Santa's head shot up. He straightened, cleared his throat, fumbled with his beard, then blustered through a pathetic string of ho-ho-ho's.

"Step right up, young lady," Santa, patting his lap, called out to the little girl at the head of the line. "Come tell Santa what you want for Christmas."

The little girl turned her face into her mother's hip and burst out crying.

"I'll go. I'll go." The boy next in line shot past the crying girl and up the two steps to land with a thud on Santa's lap. The jolly old man looked as though he was going to pass out.

"Ouch." The boy jerked his body and twisted around to glare accusingly at Santa.

Santa's beard twitched. In the middle of the fake white whiskers, pale pink lips outlined snow-white teeth. Spenser squinted for a better look. There was something very strange about this guy.

"What do you want Santa to bring you, young man?"

The boy pushed his scrunched-up nose close to the beard. "You don't smell like Santa. You smell like a, like a—"

"Ho-ho-ho! Merry Christmas!" Santa shouted loudly, drowning out the boy and starting to lift him off his lap.

"Hey, I'm supposed to give you my list." The child squirmed in outrage, holding his ground. "I want a new computer. And a bike, in-line skates, a skateboard, a basketball hoop—''

"Okay, kid. Here's your sucker. I'll see what I can do."

"I'm not finished."

Santa peered down at the boy and spoke in such a low voice that when Spenser thought he heard him say not to be a little piggy, he figured he hadn't heard right.

The boy grimaced and meekly slid off Saint Nick's lap.

"Next." Santa adjusted his belly.

Mindy hesitated, her wide eyes searching Spenser's face.

"Go ahead, honey. You have to give Santa your list."

"Come with me." She grabbed his hand and tugged hard. "You can give him your list, too."

Spenser laughed.

"Next." Santa's tone was laced with impatience.

Spenser sent the man a quick frown, then urged Mindy forward, staying close behind her.

"Well, hello. What's this pretty little girl's name?" Santa asked in his strange gruff voice.

"Mindy." Her tone had dipped a couple of octaves and her head bent shyly to the side.

"Your name is almost as pretty as you are." Santa reached out his white-gloved hands and Mindy willingly went to him, stepping up on tiptoe as he guided her onto his lap. "Do you have a list for me?"

She nodded. "It's not written down or anything."

Santa smiled. "But you remember it."

"I want my mommy to come back," she blurted out, and Spenser's gut clenched.

The smile faltered and disappeared somewhere within Santa's bushy white beard. From behind round wire glasses, a pair of striking violet eyes met Spenser's.

"And if you still have time, I'd like a Cabbage Patch doll, but I already have the one with the..."

Mindy's explanation continued but he wasn't hearing most of what she was saying. He already knew the list, had already bought most of the items on it. He wasn't even too disconcerted about her asking for her mom. He'd half expected it; he'd have been more surprised if she hadn't asked. What did unnerve him were Santa's violet eyes. He spread his legs wider and folded his arms across his chest, feeling impatient himself.

Mindy accepted a red sucker and hopped off Santa's lap. "Your turn, Daddy."

Spenser forced a smile. "The line's too long." He reached for his daughter's hand.

"No, it's not, Daddy."

"Mindy, don't you want that ice-cream cone?"

She giggled and pulled at him. "After you tell Santa what you want."

"Look, Min." Spenser hunkered down in front of her. Several people behind them complained about the holdup. "Parents don't sit on Santa's lap. This is just for kids."

"Who are you kidding? We do it all the time," a thin, graying woman behind him said. "Now get the lead out so this line can move."

Watching the stalemate between father and daughter escalate, Jill sighed. She didn't care what the guy did, as long as he did it quickly. The line wasn't getting any shorter and she had no idea how she was going to get out of here without causing a commotion. Besides, if she heard one more lousy chorus of "Jingle Bells" she was going to throw up all over Santa's nice sparkling sleigh.

She adjusted the scratchy fake beard. It was starting to give her a rash. Scanning the crowd, her eyes panned each face. There was no sign of Maury's thugs. So far. Although she'd never paid attention to the notion of having a sixth sense, something told her these guys weren't giving up.

She was in trouble. Jill just wasn't sure why. She only knew that Maury's reason for wanting to get his hands on her might be more involved than his using her as a tax shelter. Especially since all hell had broken loose after she'd made the bank deposit. Nothing unusual about that. Making the deposit was part of her job. Except there had been an awful lot of cash, and when Maury found out she'd made the deposit earlier than usual—and cashed her check—he'd been angry…angrier than she'd ever seen him.

Nerves made her skin tingle and she craned her neck for a better look down the mall. Maury never had been, nor ever would be, a love interest. He was her employer and a casual friend. And she didn't know how far his goodwill would extend.

Some of the mothers in line grunted their annoyance and two kids started crying. Jill scowled at Mindy's father. She didn't need further attention called to herself.

Leaning forward, in her best Santa voice, she whispered, "Look, mister, let's get this show on the road."

He wouldn't look at her. He said something to Mindy and smiled, before he stood and gave her ponytail a tug. His broad shoulders rose with the deep breath he took, and when he faced Jill, his smile was promptly replaced with a don't-try-anything-or-you're-toast look.

Jill tempered a wry grin. The guy was really good-looking with his dark hair and full mouth and, under other circumstances, she might have enjoyed this. But right now she needed him to sit down, make his kid happy, then move on. She patted her lap.

"Oh boy," the man muttered, pushing a hand roughly through his hair. The expression on his face as he approached made her wonder if he wanted to request his last meal.

He stopped awkwardly in front of her, then cautiously lowered himself toward her lap. Jill started to rear her head back for a better look and caught herself. He had a great butt. But Santa wasn't supposed to notice that.

He didn't settle his full weight on her, but used one of the chair arms for leverage to hold himself up—and away—from her.

"Don't be shy, sonny." She hooked an arm around his waist and pulled him against her padded middle.

"Watch it," he warned under his breath.

"I don't believe I've heard of that toy. Is there another one you want?"

The man was clearly not amused. He leaned back and for several long seconds relaxed his full weight upon her unsuspecting thighs. Jill swallowed a gasp. He had to be about six-one and nearly two hundred pounds and she thought seriously about dumping him on the floor.

He smiled. "How about a stun gun?" he asked, pitching his voice too low for small ears.

Jill smiled back. "Santa doesn't believe in guns. How about a blow-up doll?"

His eyebrows shot up. "A what?"

His expression was one of such stunned disbelief that Jill laughed, causing her padded suit to jiggle. When the man shifted against the movement, his elbow jabbed her left breast.

He blinked, slid her a suspicious look and subtly moved his elbow again.

She jerked. "Knock it off," she growled close to his ear.

Obviously startled, he lost his balance. When he tried to regain it, he grabbed for the chair arm but got a handful of her other breast instead.

"Hey..." Jill choked back a curse.

She squirmed until contact was broken and the man

nearly slid to the floor. The line of waiting children erupted into giggles, the adults, impatient sighs.

"Look..." He tried to right himself and grabbed the top of her thigh.

She opened her mouth to tell him what she thought of his roaming hands, when over his shoulder she saw two men in navy striped suits coming toward her.

Jill muttered a curse.

The man squinted at her. "What did you say?"

"All right. Off," she ordered, and when he didn't move fast enough, she used both palms to shove him and got two healthy handfuls of denim-covered flesh.

"Hey!" He jumped up, his incredulous gaze meeting hers. "What the—"

He was in the way, so she craned her neck to the side and saw that the pair she'd mistaken as part of Maury's militia had just greeted two women and a parcel of kids, and then had changed direction.

She sunk back into her throne. Giddy with relief, she looked at the stunned man edging away from her, and grinned.

Scowling back, he growled, "Buddy, I ought to punch your lights out."

Buddy? Jill wasn't sure if she should be offended or relieved that he didn't know she was a woman...or what he'd been fondling. Then she remembered she'd just gotten quite a handful herself.

"Sorry," she mumbled, trying to keep a straight face.

He started to say something else, then abruptly looked in his daughter's direction. Jill honestly didn't think anyone heard their interchange, but Mindy's gaze was wide with a mixture of curiosity and panic, and her father let out a harsh breath. His eyes suddenly narrowed under puckered eyebrows and Jill would bet her last dollar she knew what he was thinking.

Because she could almost see tomorrow's headlines, too: Father Decks Santa…Daughter Never Forgives Him.

She watched as a swift play of emotion darkened his face. Then, apparently having weighed his options, his mouth stretched into a forced smile.

Jill pressed her lips together as she quickly skimmed the sea of faces around her before calmly settling back in her throne. Still no sign of the goons.

For the time being, she knew she was safe and she let out a shaky breath.

Mindy's father's hazel eyes watched her with keen, un-nerving interest. She wasn't sure what he expected her to say or do. After all, she'd already apologized. She wished he'd just quit watching her.

She tried simply staring back but that didn't seem to faze him, so she shrugged, and mouthed, "Nice buns."

2

JILL BIT HER LIP to keep from laughing and got a nasty chunk of white whiskers caught under her teeth. She spit it out as inconspicuously as she could and adjusted her cap and beard. Her little finger caught on something and she realized that a springy tendril of her own hair had escaped from beneath the fur-rimmed cap. Quickly, she stuffed the determined corkscrew back into place.

Her hair was chronically stubborn, too curly and, adding insult to injury…red. It was going to be the death of her yet. Literally, if she weren't more careful, she thought as her gaze again swept the mall.

Seeing no sign of Maury's men, she straightened in her throne and glanced at Mindy's father. She couldn't tell if he looked more surprised or angry and she pressed her lips together to keep them from curving.

She shouldn't have antagonized him, she knew, or encouraged him to sit on her lap in the first place. But it had seemed like the sensible thing to do at the time. The entire ordeal should have taken less than a minute. It would've made Mindy happy, eliminated a possible scene, and then they could have moved on. Simple. No hassle.

But then he'd felt her up.

And worse, he still didn't realize she was a woman.

That rankled. So why did she have this sudden urge to give him a sign? To let him know she was really a she?

Her ego stepped up to answer the question and she quickly squashed the answer.

She eyed the growing line of children, heard their parents' disgruntled murmurings, and she knew she couldn't give her impulsive nature free rein. It had gotten her into trouble in the past. But not this time. She would ignore him. He would leave. She could do this.

Besides, payback was sweeter if he still thought she was a man. Let his ego get the workout. She perked up at the thought, her gaze meeting those sexy brown-green eyes.

One dark arrogant eyebrow lifted.

"Sucker," she said in a very soft feminine voice, and mentally kicked herself. Then she leaned forward to offer him the candy and indicated with her eyes that he should move on.

He left his hands at his side, one still tensed into a fist. "You're damn lucky I—"

"Daddy, is something wrong?"

When his little girl stepped up beside him, her green eyes large with concern, he relaxed and she slipped her hand into his. He touched the tip of her nose. "Nothing, Mindy. Santa was just giving me a sucker."

As he reached for the lemon-yellow lollipop, his eyes again met Jill's. They were more green than brown and they told her that he wasn't finished with her yet. A shiver skated up her spine. Not from fear, but from anticipation. Which was crazy. She planned to be out of town within the hour.

"You're nice, Santa." Mindy sagged against her father's leg, hiding half her face. "I wish you could have an ice cream with us," she mumbled, her hopeful gaze fixed on the long white beard.

Patiently rubbing his daughter's shoulder, the man smirked over her head.

Jill ignored him. "Me, too, sweetie. But all these people are waiting for me." Throwing in a ho-ho-ho, she gestured to the crowd. Out of the corner of her eye, she saw two husky, older men in dark suits hurrying in her direction.

They were still two stores away but she could tell they didn't belong to Maury...too distinguished-looking. Still, their dour expressions made her uneasy, especially with a mall security guard following close on their heels. She ducked her head for a better look, and saw a half-dressed man staggering behind them.

He should still be out cold. "Damn."

The word slipped out before Jill could stop it.

Mindy's eyes grew wider. Her father's narrowed. The woman behind them complained impatiently.

Jill ordered herself to calm down. There had to be a way out. She just needed a moment to think. "Have you heard of it, sweetie? It's a new ice-cream flavor." She slid off the throne, while glancing past them. "Damn the torpedoes or something like that." She sent them an absent smile and concentrated on the fast-approaching suits. "I think it was named after a movie."

Mindy's father let out a laugh...a short bark, actually. It wasn't a pleasant sound.

Running a finger inside her itchy fur collar, Jill stared at him. He'd been a fairly decent sport so far. And if she had to lose the Santa suit, at least Maury's men wouldn't be looking for a family. Maybe the kid and her father were her ticket out of the mall.

"I saw an ice-cream store back this way..." Jill snagged the sack of suckers she'd been passing out, then sidestepped the bag of presents leaning against the throne.

"No, it's over here," Mindy said.

"Hey, you can't leave yet," the next woman in line shouted, and that got the entire crowd grumbling.

"That store doesn't have my flavor." Jill grabbed Mindy's hand and headed in the opposite direction from the men. Her padded belly jiggled from the hasty job of stuffing the suit, and the boots, two sizes too big, felt like lead weights.

"Let go of my daughter."

The man's hand clamped painfully over Jill's shoulder, stopping her. His tone was lethal and when she lifted her gaze to his implacable one, she knew she'd hit a dead end.

"Daddy." The shock in the child's voice made them both look at her. "You can't speak that way to Santa Claus," she whispered, her eyes round with horrified indignation.

The man blinked. "Look, honey—"

"Never mind," Jill said, glancing over her shoulder and stepping away, ready to bolt. "We'll have that ice-cream cone another time."

Mindy started to cry. Her father hunkered down to her level, trying to console her.

Jill stared in dismay. It wasn't a small dainty cry like the little girl herself. It was loud and woeful and attracted far more attention than anything else could.

"Okay." Jill dropped down beside them. Desperation undermined the lower Santa pitch to her voice, which probably accounted for Mindy's prompt silence. "We'll go have that ice-cream cone. But we have to do it now."

One of the man's eyebrows rose as he peered intently at her, a speculative gleam doing all kinds of interesting things to his hazel eyes.

Mindy hiccuped and nodded, a watery smile lifting her expression.

Her father's nod was terse, reluctant. They stood.

"Spenser," he said, making no other overture. "Noah Spenser."

She acknowledged his introduction with a curt nod of her own. "Santa," she replied. "Santa Claus," and hurried them down the mall in the opposite direction of her pursuers.

SPENSER WONDERED who this woman was. Although at this point, he was just pretty damn glad that she was a woman, period. He'd figured that out when he'd mistakenly grabbed a handful of something soft and entirely too pleasant to be only padding.

He liked her hair from the sneak peek he'd gotten. It was a pretty coppery color and she had extraordinarily attractive violet eyes. But none of these things altered the fact that she was a nutcase.

Spenser shook his head. He was as screwy as she was for allowing his daughter within a football field of her. As soon as they got to the ice-cream parlor, they'd be parting company. That was for sure.

He stepped between them and took Mindy's hand.

Santa didn't seem to notice. She was too busy looking over her shoulder as she plowed through the oncoming crowd.

He briefly glanced back to see what had caught her attention and saw a parade of kids starting to follow them. They were all chattering and pointing. Santa just kept on walking as fast as those monstrous boots would allow.

"Santa, you're passing the ice-cream store," Mindy called out in a singsong voice.

"I know a better one," Santa said, flicking a glance over Mindy's head. "Where's your car?"

Spenser stopped abruptly. Two kids who'd been walking behind them ran into him. "Our car?"

"You know...tires, steering wheel, engine. It uses gas."

Santa grabbed Mindy's hand. "Let's take this exit and walk outside. It's a nice day."

"It's twenty degrees," Spenser said, and hurried to stay with his daughter. The stream of kids followed. How the hell was he going to get rid of Santa without making a scene?

"But what about our Dam-the-pedoes cone?" Mindy yanked her hand away. Standing in the middle of the thoroughfare, she crossed her arms much as he often did, except her chin stuck out at a stubborn angle that was a trait all her own.

He chuckled. He knew that stance. Santa had just met her match.

"Mindy?" Santa peered down at her. "Do you want to be my helper, or not?"

"I do," one of the kids behind them said.

"No, me, me, me." A boy, a head taller than the rest, stuck up his freckled hand. "I want to do it."

Mindy planted both hands on her hips, and pulling a long face at the other kids, said in an uncharacteristic, snippy tone, "He asked me."

"Mindy," Spenser warned.

"You can all be my helpers. Here you go." Santa upturned the bag of suckers, scattering the colorful assortment of candy into outstretched hands. Most of the sweets missed their targets and ended up strewn across the floor, which sent the pint-size crowd into a frenzy.

The kids pushed and pulled, knocking Spenser off balance and by the time he steadied himself, he saw Santa making off with his daughter. He sprinted after them and caught up just as they neared the exit.

The woman turned to look over her shoulder, but she didn't seem the least bit disturbed to find him on their tails. She obviously wasn't trying to get away from him. Her gaze wandered past him, and relief briefly flickered in her eyes before she urged Mindy through the revolving door.

Spenser pushed past the side door and met them on the other side. "Stop," he said, effectively blocking their path and putting out his hand. "Mindy, come here."

A mutinous look crossed the little girl's face and she left her hand firmly planted in Santa's white glove. "What about our ice cream?"

"Later," he said in a tone that precluded argument.

"Which way is the car?" Santa asked.

"I want that damn cone," Mindy said, and several shoppers passing by slowed down to stare, their surprise giving way to disapproval when their gazes met Spenser's.

Santa started to laugh, then cleared her throat. "For now we'll just call it...vanilla."

Mindy scrunched up her face.

"Now, where's the car?" Santa asked, casting a quick peek down the sidewalk. When a trio of laughing teenage girls came barging out of the mall, Santa spun toward the noise and nearly tripped over the ridiculously large boots on her feet.

He clamped a hand around her arm to steady her. "Are you okay?"

"Fine."

"Anything I should know about?"

"Nothing." She shook away from him, her gaze widening with forced innocence, then drifting past him toward the mall.

Santa was a liar.

He mentally weighed his options. This woman was obviously spooked about something, and although it was her business, he didn't want it involving his daughter. Ever since her mother had left, Mindy's life had been chaotic.

And Spenser was doing everything in his power to put it back to rights.

It was like walking a tightrope sometimes, trying to reassure her and not spoil her at the same time. He didn't always know if he was doing the right thing, no matter how hard he tried. But he couldn't afford to be a part-time father anymore. No excuses. No more letting his career come first. He'd gotten his wake-up call. Now, he was going to be daddy for the long haul.

"It's cold, Daddy," Mindy said, shivering. "Can we go to the car?"

"Lead the way," Santa said cheerfully, then craned her neck to check out the exiting shoppers.

"Not you." Spenser said to Santa, and took Mindy's hand.

His daughter's eyes rounded. "But Santa's coming to dinner."

"Mindy, I don't think Santa has time," Spenser said, glancing at her to back him up.

She dragged her gaze away from the door and turned to look at them. Behind the round wire-rimmed glasses, her violet eyes brightened. "Of course I do."

He blinked. "Excuse me?"

"But we really have to get a move on. I have, uh, presents to make or something. Yeah, at the North Pole."

Briefly, he closed his eyes and passed a weary hand over his face. Mindy tugged at his hand. "Daddy, I'm freezing."

"You really shouldn't keep the kid out in the cold," Santa said and had the nerve to add a disapproving cluck.

He gave her a bland look, then smiled at Mindy. "Okay, let's get you warm and toasty."

He wasn't surprised that Santa followed close on their heels. When she tried to take Mindy's other hand, he wedged himself between them. He didn't want his daughter in close range of this psycho Santa. She was as nutty as the fruitcake his mother insisted on baking each year.

Over Mindy's head, he whispered, "We need to talk."

The woman frowned. "We can do that when we get home."

Home? If not the nuttiest, she was possibly the nerviest woman he'd ever met. "That's what we need to talk about."

"Oh," she said, looking as if she'd been caught raiding the cookie jar.

A reluctant smile tugged at his lips. "Everyone calls me Spenser. What about you? Have you got another name besides Santa?"

"Jill," she said after hesitating. "But call me Santa in front of anyone else." She tried to look nonchalant, but Spenser noted the way her gaze quickly and precisely cut through the aisles between the cars. "Silent Night" played from a nearby car radio. He had a feeling he was in for anything but.

She was paying more attention to her surroundings than she was to them, so when they neared the car, he made a sharp right turn, hoping he'd lose her. She tripped, trying to stay with them, and he ended up catching her arm.

For a moment she sagged against him, their bodies meeting from midthigh to shoulder. There was no padding there in her Santa suit and he could feel her warmth through the red crushed velvet. She lingered only a matter of seconds but the contact was enough to send an arrow of unease right to his gut.

Jill pulled away and he used his newly freed hand to tug at the collar of his jacket. This was crazy. He wasn't a whimsical man. He was a jet pilot, for God's sake. He believed in science, in tangibles. Not loony notions of cosmic connections.

She touched his arm and he jerked. A line of tension was etched between her eyebrows. "Is the car much farther? It's hard to walk in these boots and I'm getting a doozy of a blister."

"We're almost there, aren't we, Daddy?" Mindy smiled up at him. She looked happy, happier than he'd seen her in a long time.

"Yup, so we can slow down," he said, and Jill looked as though she wanted to argue. Instead, she glanced over her shoulder and eyed a group of weary shoppers returning to their cars.

Okay, so he already knew that she was in trouble. So why did he care? Whatever her problem was, it wasn't his business. In fact, this was a good time to get rid of her.

He cleared his throat, about to tell her that it was time for them to part company, when her eyes briefly met his. Fear and vulnerability shadowed them, surprising him, making the words stick like peanut butter to the roof of his mouth.

He let out a long steady breath and said to Jill, "Why don't you lean on me?"

She blinked. "Dressed like this? Won't that look funny?"

"Probably."

She laughed and took his arm when he presented it to her. "Geez, where's Rudolph when you need him?"

"He ran off with the Easter Bunny. Watch that ice patch."

She leaned into him as she scooted around the frozen puddle. Her weight felt welcome against him, and catching a whiff of something floral, he breathed deeply. When she cleared the icy ground and shifted some of her weight away from him, he felt a sense of loss.

"Here we are," Mindy said, her voice quavering from

the cold. She'd already undone the top of her jacket and he fought the urge to snap it back in place. If she wanted it fastened again, she'd do it herself. He had to learn to let her.

He didn't understand her new streak of rebellious independence. He wasn't sure if it had more to do with her age or her mother's desertion. Her counselor said it was a little of both. Spenser merely recognized the irony. Now that he was around, she didn't seem to need him as much. While all he wanted to do was smother her with attention. But he was learning. One step at a time.

He unlocked the car doors and quickly got her inside.

"Don't worry. I won't stay for dinner," Jill whispered once Mindy was inside and out of earshot.

"I wasn't worried."

"Liar." Through the beard's mouth opening, he caught a peek of those pink lips stretching across her teeth.

Pursing his mouth, he stared into her eyes. "Interesting subject to bring up."

The grin vanished. "Shall we go?"

"Why should I take you anywhere?"

She wrinkled her nose. "In the spirit of the season?"

"Are you in trouble?"

"Not exactly," she said, and when he lifted an eyebrow, she added, "It's a long story."

He was probably going to regret this, he thought with a weary shake of his head.

"We've got time. Dinner isn't for a couple of hours," he said, then swung open the back door for her.

3

THE SPENSERS HAD a nice house. It was a two-story brick colonial with several tall slender pines flanking its corners. A three-car garage was unattached to the right, but Jill was relieved when Spenser skipped it and pulled the car up a wide circular driveway, placing her side of the car close to the front entrance.

Mindful of the blisters that seemed to have multiplied on her feet during the short drive, Jill slid out of the Ford Taurus and eyed the well-kept neighborhood while she waited for Spenser to disengage Mindy from her seat belt. The entire setting was so nice and middle-class and average it was kind of spooky.

Although similar in size, each house was different. English Tudors blended with colonials and Cape Cods. Most of them had decorated trees in their spacious front yards, and festive wreaths hanging on their doors. And although there was still at least an hour left before dark, a couple of houses already had their Christmas lights turned on, the strings of red and white draping from the eaves, or spiraling around pole lamps, making them look like giant candy canes.

Clusters of evergreens kept the landscape from looking too winter-bleak and most of the lawns were still semi-green, except for scattered patches of snow from a fall several days earlier.

Jill glanced up at the sky. She hoped the weather held

up until she got out of town, although she wasn't too worried. In the nearly three years she'd lived in southern Michigan, she'd found that snow was hardly a given even this late in December.

The thought stopped her. Had she really been here this long? Limping toward the front stoop, she mentally calculated exactly how long it had been since she'd pulled into town on a whim and ended up working at Maury's travel agency.

Three years. Mind-boggling. It was the longest she'd lived anywhere. A year and a half in one spot was the old record for her. No wonder she was getting a tad antsy. Even if Maury hadn't started in again on this nonsense about getting married, she probably would have been shoving off soon, anyway.

Reminded of him, she envisioned his henchmen, and with a shiver, she saw yesterday's events replay themselves in her mind. Nothing particularly different had happened that day, until she'd deposited the briefcase full of cash. What stuck in her mind the most was how insanely angry Maury had been upon her return from the bank. After that, everything went haywire at the usually peaceful travel agency, with a slew of phone calls coming in and going out. Within an hour, his eccentric family and the goons had appeared.

And for the first time, Jill had seen the calm, cool, arrogant Maury begin to sweat.

Last Christmas when he had proposed, she'd told him he was crazy. He'd called the judge anyway, and she'd taken a train trip north until after the holidays. By the time she'd returned, all was forgotten and forgiven.

The whole episode had seemed like a joke. It certainly hadn't been a big deal. Leaving for the holidays had meant nothing to her. She never celebrated Christmas. She sent her brother and father each a gift if she knew at which base they were stationed. And Maury's proposal...it had nothing to do with love and everything to do with a joint tax return.

But this year seemed more complicated. She didn't know why, which was probably the worst part. She hated not knowing. The only thing she did know was that shortly after his family had arrived yesterday, an agitated Maury informed her that the wedding had to take place as soon as possible. There was no question he meant it this time. That's when Jill had packed a hasty bag and split.

She'd made it as far as the mall. The fact that Maury had her followed confirmed the gravity of the situation, whatever that was.

She shivered again as she stepped into the shadow of a stately pine guarding the entry door.

"Cold?" Spenser moved in beside her.

She cast a reflexive glance past him, then hugged herself. The red velvety material was thin, but that didn't account for her sudden chill. "A little."

He followed her gaze toward the empty street, then leveled his eyes with hers. "I'll start a fire right away."

She looked away. "I'm not staying long."

He didn't say anything, but she felt the weight of his stare while he slid the key into the lock, then pushed open the door.

"After you, ladies," he said, and Mindy giggled as she led the way into the house.

Lights flooded the foyer just as Jill felt something at her back. She jumped and twisted to find Spenser's arm stretching behind her. His fingers slid from the light switch, grazing her left shoulder.

"Something wrong?" he asked. As if to make a point, he turned to look outside before closing the door.

Jill ignored him. He couldn't know she was worried

about being followed, and she wasn't going to let him goad her into telling him. In a half hour, it wouldn't matter. She'd be gone.

Mindy stripped off her jacket, and after Spenser hung it up, he turned to Jill. "Can I take your...beard?"

She laughed. The thought was tempting. Her neck and chin itched beneath the scratchy beard, and the crushed-velvet suit clung to her clammy skin. She wished she could shuck the entire getup, but she wasn't about to walk around in her bra and panties.

And then she caught Mindy's wide-eyed appraisal. Jill's gaze darted to Spenser's and she signaled with her eyes for him to be careful about what he said.

"My beard?" she asked with mock dismay. At the last moment, she remembered to throw in a ho-ho-ho. "That would hurt."

He smiled. It was a nice smile. His teeth were movie-star white against his clean-shaven face, and an attractive groove appeared in his right cheek. "Mindy understands that you're only Santa's helper. Kind of like an elf."

"Right." Jill plucked the spectacles off the bridge of her nose. Believing in Santa was a waste of time. Good thing her father's drunken army buddy had set her straight at an early age.

Mindy's forehead creased and she pursed her thin lips. "Daddy, is our elf a boy or a girl helper?"

Spenser's eyebrows drew together as he pretended to gravely consider his daughter's question, except a small twitch pulled at one corner of his mouth. "Gee, Min, I'm not sure."

Then he folded his arms, and watching Jill with an amused gaze, leaned back as though waiting for the show to begin.

Jill fumbled with the beard, feeling oddly as if she was

about to perform a striptease. Although it wasn't a particularly sensual look he was giving her, she caught herself watching his full mouth and experienced a strange shiver of anticipation.

"Well?" he prompted with a challenging lift of his chin.

Before giving the situation another thought, she ripped off the beard, twirled it in the air and threw it at him. It landed on his shoulder.

He barely moved. His gaze fell on the beard, and slowly straightening, he dragged it off his shoulder and looked up at her, his eyebrows lifted. "And with no music. I'm impressed."

"Wow." Mindy sidled up to her. "You *are* a girl."

"Last time I looked." Jill's smile hastily faltered when she realized what she'd just said. She stole a glance at Spenser and cringed. His attention had strayed to her breasts. She bit back a tart remark.

He blinked. "Mindy, go get washed up."

"But Daddy—"

"Mindy."

"Okay." She turned to Jill. "You won't leave, will you?"

"Not yet."

"You have to have dinner with us first, then maybe you could spend the night, then maybe I could call my friends, then—"

"Mindy." Spenser's voice was stern, and then he added, "We'll discuss this after you're cleaned up."

She let out a long-suffering sigh, then did an abrupt about-face and stomped down the hall toward the back of the house.

"Let's go into the family room and get those boots off you." Spenser wasn't smiling as he led Jill into a large wood-paneled room with a stone fireplace and a massive burgundy-leather couch.

One wall was nothing but bookshelves crammed to capacity with an assortment of paperbacks and hardcover books. Several of the bigger books were on aircraft design, Jill noted as she claimed a mauve and cream-colored wingback chair. She surveyed the rest of the room, conscious of how differently her apartment was furnished. These people actually used end tables instead of moving boxes.

Homes like this, with real furniture, looked nothing like the number of apartments she'd had. Being reminded of how the other half lived always came as a little bit of a jolt to her system.

Spenser continued toward the fireplace, and withdrawing a box of long matches from behind the brass fireplace tools, he struck a flame and lit the kindling he'd already had waiting.

"Nice house," Jill said. The room was tidy and well-kept, almost too neat for having a child living here.

Behind her, near the window, was the Christmas tree. She twisted around to get a better look, but her gaze automatically shot past the tree through the large plate glass. The drapes were only partially drawn and she was afforded an excellent view of the street. No cars. No goons. Only Christmas lights. Relief surged through her, surprising her, because she hadn't realized she was still this tense. Briefly she thought about asking Spenser to draw the drapes, but discarded the idea with equal brevity. He was suspicious enough, as it was. And she was being unnecessarily paranoid. She hoped.

Instead, she concentrated on the tree, and smiled. From midtree to the floor, the live spruce glowed with Mindy's handiwork. Bright-colored streams of paper garland were draped haphazardly from one limb to the next. A hilarious assortment of paper-doll cutouts danced and fluttered among the sweet-smelling branches.

The top half of the tree, the part only Spenser could reach, was decorated with unimaginative blue Christmas balls and a token splatter of silver tinsel, and she had a sudden crazy urge to strip off the sterile ornaments and rearrange them.

The impulse surprised and irritated her. It reminded her of times better left forgotten. Times she'd spent as a lonely kid, standing outside life's circle, never living anywhere long enough to make friends or even decorate a Christmas tree.

Sure, she'd seen more of the world by the time she was ten than most people saw in a lifetime, but even at an early age she'd figured there was more to life than living on army bases. Her father never turned down a single transfer, even though, for all his effort, he never made it past the rank of sergeant. And no amount of begging and pleading ever changed his mind.

It wasn't so bad, though. Generally she'd had a few days notice to say goodbye to teachers and a few of the kids at school. Because the piece of yellow paper always tipped her off. Her dad would walk in with it in his hand, smiling, and tell Jill and her brother that this time for sure he'd make sergeant major. But he never did. He got drunk instead.

And then they would pack up all over again and, as always, the yellow paper would sit on the counter until the moving vans showed up to take their things to the next base.

That was probably why Jill hated the color. Rarely ever touched it, except at the travel agency where she worked and only when documents needed to be filled out in triplicate. And then it still bugged her to have to tear off that last yellow sheet. It reminded her of the nights she'd cried herself to sleep because Santa wasn't going to know where she was that Christmas.

Nor would her mother.

But that was before she realized that neither of them had been looking for her, after all.

Pushing the past aside, Jill gave Spenser a bland look. "Nice tree."

He'd settled across from her on the couch and was watching her. "Ready to get those boots off?"

"I was thinking maybe that's not such a good idea. I might not be able to get them back on."

"Maybe they shouldn't go back on."

She bristled at his tone even though he was probably right; her feet were aching beyond belief. But he sounded as if he were speaking to Mindy. "And how do you suggest I return to the mall? Barefoot?"

"Somehow, I didn't think you'd be anxious to go back."

"Why would you say that?" She lifted her hand to tuck a strand of hair behind her ear, a nervous habit she'd picked up as a kid, then realized that she was still wearing the Santa cap.

He leaned farther back, sprawling out on the couch as if he owned the place...which, of course, he did. "Come on, Jill. What's going on? What kind of trouble are you in?"

"That's personal," she said. "Not that I'm in any trouble."

"It's personal to me when you drag my daughter into it."

Jill caught her breath. She hadn't thought if it that way. Except she hadn't placed them in any danger. It was her Maury was trying to hitch up with. Plus, they hadn't been followed, and Maury would never think of looking for her in a neighborhood like this. Would he? Unease made her shift in the chair.

"Really. You have nothing to worry about. Besides, I'll be on my way as soon as Mindy comes back."

He eyed the Santa getup. "How do you propose to do that?"

"A taxi."

He raised his eyebrows in amused disbelief. "What are you going to do? Promise the driver he'll get his fare in a wrapped package under the tree?"

"Very funny." She patted the area above her chest. Funny, she didn't feel anything. But of course she wouldn't feel a folded twenty. "I *always* have cab fare."

"Never know when you need to make a fast getaway, huh?"

"Right." She frowned, sniffed. "I mean, no. A girl should always be prepared. That's all."

"Right," he echoed, the amusement on his face mingling with suspicion. "So why this little side trip, just to turn around and go back to the mall?"

Jill shrugged. "To please Mindy."

His hazel eyes narrowed. "If you tell me what's really going on, maybe I can help."

Sighing, Jill pulled the cap off her head. Immediately, a riot of curls sprang to life. She sighed again, this time it was a little more heartfelt. Nothing short of a blizzard was ever going to subdue this hair.

"Okay, I'll give it to you straight," she said and looked Spenser in the eyes. Except he wasn't looking back. Not eye level, anyway. His gaze was fixed on the top of her head. "Not a word about the color," she warned.

"What?" He hesitated, squinting a little. "I like auburn."

"Auburn?" That was a nice way of saying red. Frowning, she looked up. Then she plucked a thick strand between her thumb and forefinger, her eyes crossing as she drew it down for a look. "Oh, yeah. Auburn." She'd forgotten she'd been to the hairdresser's yesterday. "Anyway..."

He was frowning now, his gaze aimed somewhere above hers.

"What is it?" she asked, her patience slipping.

"Nothing."

Gingerly, she lifted a hand to pat the top of her head.

With obvious effort, he dragged his attention to her face. "You were about to tell me about this trouble you're in."

Great. How was she supposed to concentrate when something funky was happening with her hair? "I'm not in any trouble," she snapped. "Santa was."

"Santa," he repeated, nodding sagely, patiently, and she had the sudden urge to smack him.

"Yeah. He got drunk, passed out and there was going to be a whole bunch of disappointed kiddies. So I stepped in." That was a great explanation. Partly true, too. She settled back, proud of herself, and patted her hair again. It didn't feel different.

"Very commendable, but that doesn't explain why you keep looking over your shoulder."

"Because I didn't tell anyone. I just did it."

He inclined his head slightly forward. "And?"

"I think I saw mall security and they were coming at me." She shrugged. "Maybe they thought I'd mugged the man."

"Why would they think that?"

"What would you think if you saw some man stripped down to his long johns sprawled out on the floor?"

He drew a hand down his face, covering his mouth for a moment. When he let his palm drop to his thigh, she saw that he was trying to stifle a grin. "You left him in his underwear?"

"He didn't fit in my clothes."

"Ah, of course."

She nodded, pleased. "But once I get back and explain, I'm sure everything will be okay."

"Think so? You deserted an entire line of children and their not-too-happy parents."

Jill bit her lip. "I am sorry about that."

His gaze drew to her mouth, staying a second too long, and again she felt that odd little shiver shimmy in her chest. His hand seemed to make a reflexive move on his thigh, and he dragged his palm down his jeans to a spot above his knee. He stopped, his long lean fingers kneading the muscles there.

She swallowed. There was something happening to the air. Maybe he'd let the fire get too hot, or turned the thermostat too high. It was getting a little hard to breathe. The suit started itching again.

"All clean." Mindy stood at the door, her hands out.

They both jumped, and Jill wasn't sure why she felt guilty all of a sudden. She pasted on a bright smile. "Hi, sweetie."

Mindy's eyes narrowed, then widened. "What's wrong with your hair?"

Jill's hand flew to her head and she looked helplessly at Spenser.

He burst out laughing.

4

JILL GRABBED her cap and jammed it back onto her head. But right before she did, she saw the telltale signs of auburn tint staining the fake white-fur rim.

Abruptly, she stood. "May I use your bathroom?"

Spenser cleared his throat. "Down the hall and to the left."

"But what's all that—"

"Later, Mindy," her father said, cutting her off. "Come help me make some hot chocolate."

"Before dinner? Wow." Mindy's eyes rounded and, grinning impishly, she scooted out the door ahead of Jill.

"Take your time," Spenser told Jill as he started to follow his daughter. "Help yourself to whatever you need in the cabinets. Yell if you want anything else."

"How about an extra-large bandage?" Jill rubbed her aching temple. When he frowned in confusion, she added, "Big enough for a wounded ego."

He laughed. "Stick around. Kids have a way of taking care of ego problems."

Stick around? Not on her life. The sooner she got out of town the better. She watched him disappear through the door that presumably separated the dining room from the kitchen. From the other side, she heard Mindy's excited high-pitched chatter, and she grinned as she hurried in the direction of the bathroom.

But as soon as she faced herself in the mirror and pulled

off the Santa cap, her smile faded. Not only had the hair tint bled into the cap, but several tiny lines streamed down her forehead toward her eyebrows, leaving a faded ring around her head.

Quickly she unpinned her hair and as it fell to her shoulders, she saw the varying splotches of red patterns where the tint had bled. She looked more like a clown than like Santa.

This couldn't be happening. She took a deep breath. The collar of the Santa suit felt unbearably tight, and she unfastened the top button before gripping both sides of the sink and leaning in for a closer look at herself.

Even her cheeks were slightly smudged with red, a small hive-looking welt was forming near her jaw. She'd had her hair tinted before. Nothing like this had ever happened. Maybe she was allergic to the Santa suit, she thought, and leaned back so she could scratch her elbow. And then she scratched her left thigh.

She made a wry face at her reflection. Power of suggestion, that's all that was. She scrubbed at the red trails on her face and managed to at least fade them. Squinting closer, she realized that the problem wasn't her hair color at all.

"Everything okay?" Spenser's voice came from the other side of the door.

"I think something's wrong with the suit," she said and unfastened another button in order to inspect her chest.

"Maybe you'd better take it off."

"I'm not wearing anything underneath."

Silence hung in the air.

"I mean, of course I'm wearing *something*. Just not anything I'd wear in mixed company."

"Do you want a robe?"

Jill frowned at the red splotches beginning to form on

her chest. She couldn't return to the mall in a robe, and it was beginning to look as if she wasn't going to go anywhere in this suit, either. She peeled the red velvet flap farther back. The color had bled into her white cotton bra, turning it pink.

And her emergency twenty-dollar bill was nowhere to be seen. Slipping her hand inside the cup, she patted around and came up with nothing except damp skin. She let out a shriek.

"Jill?"

When she didn't answer, Spenser burst through the door. His expression panicked, he asked, "Are you okay?"

One hand still feeling inside her bra, her gaze flew to his and she said, "It's gone."

His gaze narrowed before lowering to her chest, and he blinked. Slowly he asked, "What's gone?"

Realizing how exposed she was, she withdrew her hand and pulled the flaps of the suit together.

His eyes met hers, his pupils dilating as he tugged at the collar of his shirt. "Everything looked in order to me."

"Very funny. Now, would you get out of here so I can look for it?"

"I still don't understand what—"

Jill pushed him back over the threshold, and ignoring his look of surprise, she closed the door before he could finish. With a loud click, she locked the door. She started to peel back the flap once more, and feeling a touch of remorse for manhandling him, she called, "I'll be out in a minute."

Spenser didn't seem put off by her, if his deep rumbling laugh was any indication. "My offer of a robe still stands."

She stared at the wedge of skin she'd exposed. The welts were scattered, but it was clear she was having some kind of reaction. "Okay, or maybe a T-shirt, if you have one."

"I might even have a straitjacket," he said, his voice already fading.

She chuckled in spite of herself, then finished unfastening the suit. As soon as she shrugged out of it, she unhooked her bra and pulled it off.

No twenty-dollar bill was in sight, but a key bounced off the sea-green tile floor.

She'd almost forgotten about the locker she'd rented at the mall, but quickly grabbed the key, laying it safely on the counter. It was actually more important than the money. She'd stashed all her belongings for the next week in the locker, her purse included.

After thoroughly searching inside the jacket, she pinched along the elastic waistband of the enormous pants. No luck. The money wasn't there. Her heart sinking, she started to repeat the process when she heard the knock at the door.

From outside in the hall, Spenser cleared his throat. "I have a robe, T-shirt, sweatpants and a white flag."

Jill grabbed a towel off the rack and tucked it around her. She inched open the door, stuck out her arm and peeked through the narrow opening. Only his shoulder, one hand and a denim-covered leg were visible as he draped the clothes over her arm.

"Mindy has hot chocolate made, so come to the kitchen when you're changed. It's down the hall to the left."

"Spenser?"

As soon as she'd drawn the clothes inside and started to close the door, he'd backed away. But he stopped at the sound of her voice and, through the crack between the door and the frame, she peered down at one scuffed boot.

"Thanks."

"No problem."

"I'm sorry if I seemed short with you before."

"I shouldn't have barged in on you."

The towel started to slip and she hiked it back up to keep her breasts covered. "Spenser?"

"Yeah?"

"You didn't see anything, did you?" She thought she heard him smile, which of course was ridiculous. Although no more ridiculous than why she'd asked that stupid question. If he had seen more than he should have, it would have been wise for her to have ignored it. "Never mind," she said and shut the door with a definitive click.

"Jill?"

She clutched the towel tighter, stared at the closed door and thought about not answering. "Yeah?"

"Let's put it this way," he said, his voice lowering. "At least I didn't notice your hair."

SPENSER STUCK the casserole his mother had left for them into the oven to warm and pulled salad fixings out of the refrigerator. He sniffed a red pepper, poked at a cucumber and made a face. Quickly, he rearranged his expression and glanced over to see if Mindy had spotted his reaction. But she was too busy ogling Jill's cooling mug of chocolate to notice.

One of the hardest things about playing double-time father was practicing what he preached. That meant eating green things other than Life Savers candy. He dumped everything on a cutting board and tried not to shudder.

"Can I help?"

He looked up to find Jill grinning at him. Her hair looked fine now, hanging in damp ringlets just past her shoulders, his white T-shirt doing an admirable job of hugging small but perfectly round breasts. Without warning, the earlier image of her half-dressed flashed in his mind and he fumbled the cucumber, nearly letting it fall to the floor.

Her grin widened and for an insane moment he thought

she knew what he'd been thinking. But then her eyes, gleaming with amusement, pointedly surveyed the assortment of vegetables, and she said, "Salad. Your favorite, huh?"

"Sure. Isn't it yours?"

"Cheeseburgers, French fries, hold the tomato, lettuce and pickles. They're far too healthy for me."

Mindy giggled. Spenser frowned at Jill.

Her eyebrows shot up. "What?"

From behind Mindy, he inclined his head meaningfully toward his daughter. "We love salads in this house."

Jill's lips curved again as comprehension dawned, and she nodded. "With lots of cucumbers and...and... radishes."

"Radishes?" Mindy wrinkled her nose. "Those red things?"

"Don't push it," he mouthed over his daughter's head, then said aloud, "If you really want to help, you can cut up these vegetables."

"Sure. I can handle that." Frowning at the knife, she accepted it awkwardly.

Spenser moved to the sink and withdrew three water glasses from the right-hand cupboard. "Is everything okay with you?"

"It will be. Cheap crushed velvet and I don't seem to get along," she said, eyeing the trio of tumblers with misgiving.

"Wine or juice with dinner?" he asked.

She stared down at the red pepper she was methodically slicing into small slivers. "I need to ask you a favor."

"Shoot."

"Remember the emergency money I always have on me?"

He nodded, and her gaze darted to him when she didn't hear an answer.

"It's gone. I need to borrow cab fare," she said and returned her attention to the pepper. "I know you don't know me, but I promise I'm good for it."

"I can do that."

Her shoulders visibly relaxed. "I'll mail it back to you tomorrow."

"Why mail it?"

Her gaze flicked toward him, then skittered away. "I'm leaving town tonight."

Mindy sighed loudly and they both turned to look at her. She'd climbed onto a stool and was sitting at the butcher-block island in the center of the kitchen, staring at Jill. "You don't look like Santa's helper anymore. You look like a regular girl. Your hair doesn't even look funny now."

Jill laughed and her entire face lit up. She looked young all scrubbed up the way she was and Spenser wondered how old she was. He also wondered why she was in a hurry to leave town.

"Mindy, why don't you go set the table?" He lifted her off the stool and handed her some napkins and silverware.

"Can I call my friends and tell them that Santa's helper is having dinner with us?" she asked while trying to balance everything in her small hands.

"I don't know, honey." He glanced at Jill, who cringed. "You set the table and then we'll see."

As soon as Mindy trudged out of the kitchen, Jill said, "I'm sorry I can't stay."

"You have a plane to catch?"

She shook her head and concentrated on transferring the cut vegetables into a bowl.

"A train?"

This time the shake was curt.

"Why don't you tell me what's going on, Jill?" he repeated. "Maybe I can help you."

She turned toward him, her chin lifting at a stubborn angle, and he knew she wasn't going to tell him a thing.

"Daddy, Daddy!" Mindy came running from the dining room, her ponytail whipping across flushed cheeks. "Look outside."

Jill's knife dropped with a clang and she turned stricken eyes toward the windows above the sink.

Spenser frowned. "Slow down, Min, you know you're not supposed to run in the house. What's going on?"

A grin swept her face. "It's snowing!" She held up her hands a foot apart. "The flakes are this big."

"That big, huh?" He laughed. "I'll have to see that. How about you, Jill? You want to have a look?"

Obvious relief returned some color to her pale cheeks and he saw her shoulders sag with the deep breath she exhaled. A smile touched the corners of her mouth. "Sure. Let's see those giant flakes."

It was a strange reaction for someone who was trying to get out of town. Unless she was planning on leaving by snowmobile. But he already knew Jill was worried about something more important than how much snow would be accumulating. He just didn't know what.

They all filed out to the family room where the large plate-glass window gave them a perfect view of the front yard and the big fluffy snowflakes falling at an alarming rate. The circular driveway was already covered with white, and only sporadic patches of green showed in the yard.

"Daddy, can I go out and play? I promise to wear my mittens and everything."

"Maybe after dinner."

Jill stared transfixed. "Was it supposed to do this today?"

"Anywhere from three to five inches."

From the kitchen, the oven timer buzzed. She blinked and looked at him. "I'd better get a cab while I still can."

"I'm not sure that's an option." Shrugging, he tugged Mindy away from the window. "Cab service in this town isn't reliable even under ideal conditions. After dinner, I'll drive you to the mall."

"But then, when can I go out and play?" Mindy stuck out her chin, her eyes narrowing on Jill. "You promised you'd stay."

"Okay, everyone in the kitchen and we'll serve ourselves from there." Spenser wasn't in the mood for one of Mindy's mini tantrums. He had to decide what to do about Jill. "While we eat, we'll discuss what we're going to do."

"I'm going to try calling for a cab," Jill said as she followed them to the kitchen. "There's no need for you and Mindy to go out in this weather."

Spenser chuckled. "I fly planes in worse weather than this. Believe me, it's no problem."

"My dad used to fly big jets, bigger than this whole house, bigger than this whole street," Mindy said as she reached for her plate off the butcher-block island. "But he doesn't anymore."

"Don't forget your salad, young lady." He dished her up a healthy portion of lettuce and cucumbers, knowing that would take Mindy's mind off spilling his life history.

"Hey, that's too much," Mindy said. Squinting at the plate, she took it before he could add any more.

"Go sit down and I'll bring your casserole."

She scampered off toward the dining room and he turned to Jill, who was watching him with undisguised interest. "You wanna get your own salad?"

"I'm getting out of here before I have to eat that stuff." She leaned over the wooden island and cocked her head to the side. Her coppery ringlets caught the light and made her hair shimmer like liquid fire. "So, you're a pilot?"

"Yeah."

"But you don't fly anymore?"

He passed her a plate. "A few token pieces of lettuce won't kill you."

She pursed her lips a moment, her eyebrows furrowed over those brilliant violet eyes, and then she smiled and he knew she had blessedly decided to drop the subject. "Why don't you get me the phone book so you can go eat with Mindy?"

"Can't do that."

Wariness clouded her face. "I don't understand."

He smiled. "I have to give her time to unload some of her veggies." When Jill's eyebrows raised in disbelief, he added, "Come on, didn't you do that when you were a kid? Ditch your vegetables when no one was looking."

She shook her head, the confused look on her face plain. "I didn't have to."

"Didn't your mom make you eat all your green stuff?" he teased.

"I didn't have a mom." She shrugged. "The casserole is getting cold."

"Dad," Mindy yelled from the dining room. "Santa Jill. I'm all by myself."

"I guess she did her unloading already," Jill said, a grin returning to her lips. "Go eat with her. I'll be in after I use the phone."

Spenser studied her while she yanked the Yellow Pages she'd found out from under the phone in the corner. The smart thing for him to do would be to let her go. He had enough to worry about, what with getting ready for Christmas and keeping the house in order while their house-keeper, Celia, was visiting her kids for the holidays.

He didn't know Jill, certainly didn't owe her a thing. And if his instinct was in working order, her brand of trouble wasn't what he needed right now.

That's what he was going to do, he decided, reaching for the Italian dressing. Give her some money, let her get in a cab, wish her a nice life. He unscrewed the top and drowned his salad with the oily blend. He didn't need to know what kind of trouble she was in or why she'd been masquerading as Santa Claus.

He didn't even need to know why she'd grown up without a mother.

Spenser set down the salad dressing and glanced over at her again. If she had looked young before, she'd looked all of twelve when she'd calmly announced that she had no mother. There was no self-pity or sadness in her clear violet eyes, or anything he could put his finger on, but he knew deep in his gut that she wasn't as blasé about her situation as she pretended. Maybe he was projecting the angst of his own daughter onto Jill. He didn't know. All he knew was that a strange and undeniable tug of sympathy had just wiped out his appetite.

Watching her run her finger down a column of numbers and pick up the phone with her other hand, he used a wooden spoon to dish up three plates of the cheesy casserole.

Without the Santa suit, she was slightly built. Her arms were slender, her skin pale…her hands bare. He blinked before studying her slim, unmarked fingers closer.

It never occurred to him that she might be married until this moment. She looked so young. But maybe she was running away from an abusive husband; her skittishness would certainly fit that possible scenario. No ring and no sign that she'd worn one recently suggested otherwise.

Sighing with disgust, he threw the spoon into the casserole dish.

Who the hell was he kidding? He wasn't going to let her take a cab. Yes, she did have to leave—there was no question about that—but he'd take her to the mall himself, make sure she got there safely.

"Look, Jill—"

The doorbell rang, cutting him off and snagging Jill's attention better than he had.

Her startled eyes met his and widened with alarm, reminding him that he was a fool to get involved with this woman and her problems.

"I'll get it," Mindy called out.

"No, you don't, young lady." Spenser pushed off from the island, ready to sprint after his daughter.

"It's only Grandma," she called. "I see her car."

His mother, again? He let out a curse. It was low and muffled but loud enough to net a devilish grin from Jill.

He rammed a hand through his hair. "She's going to drive me nuts," he muttered on his way out of the kitchen.

Mindy had done exactly what he'd instructed her at least a hundred times not to do without him. She'd opened the front door. His mother was already barging in over the threshold, a foil-wrapped pan in her hands.

"How's my best girl?" She bent over to press a bright pink ring of lipstick on Mindy's cheek.

"Hi, Grandma, is that dessert?" Mindy asked, rubbing her cheek and smearing the pink stuff all the way down to her jaw.

"Mother, what are you doing driving in the snow?"

She cast a critical eye toward the family room. "You

have to eat, don't you? Your Christmas tree is leaning slightly to the left. I'll fix it in a moment.''

"You already brought us a casserole for tonight's dinner, remember?''

"Don't use that tone with me, Noah Aaron. Someone has to take care of you while Celia is away. Now, put this pot roast in the refrigerator.'' She shoved the pan at him, then pushed back the hood from her perfectly styled blond hair.

When she started to tug off her fur-lined boots, Spenser's heart sank. He was in for a long evening. He loved his mom, but she didn't know when to quit. And ever since his wife left, she hadn't let up. Now with the holidays and Celia's absence, he was no doubt in for a double dose of Margaret Spenser's smothering.

She handed him her coat, Mindy her boots. "After I tidy up a bit, I'll fix…''

Her voice trailed off as she looked past him, toward the dining room, and by the stunned expression on her face, he didn't need to turn around to know she'd spotted Jill. Standing in the foyer, his mother had a clear view of the kitchen door…and his unexpected guest.

Heaving a weary sigh, he hung up her coat, then braced himself to introduce the two women. "Mom, I'd like you to meet—''

He stopped. He had no idea what Jill's last name was. Fortunately, his mother didn't seem to be listening. She'd started for the kitchen, and bless her obsessive-compulsive nature, she'd stopped to straighten the silverware on the dining-room table.

After slanting a fork a centimeter to the right, she raised two perfectly arched eyebrows. "You were saying?''

He couldn't do this. He couldn't face ten days of her

straightening every picture, dusting each ornament, hovering over them like a chef over a chocolate soufflé.

Clearing his throat, he grabbed Mindy's hand and gave it a small warning tug as Jill stepped tentatively into the doorway and smiled. "Mother, I'd like you to meet our new housekeeper, Jill."

His mother's eyebrows shot higher.

He shrugged helplessly. "Jill Claus."

5

JILL FIGURED she hadn't heard correctly. Surely Spenser hadn't just introduced her as their new housekeeper. She smiled at Mindy's grandmother and waited for him to finish the introduction. The woman didn't smile back.

"Does that mean she's staying?" Mindy asked, her eyes wide with excitement. She pulled free of her father and flung herself at Jill.

Jill didn't know quite what to do, so she dropped to one knee and patted Mindy's back. Then she shot Spenser a dirty look.

"What happened to Celia?" the older woman demanded.

Spenser ignored her, his gaze fastened on Jill, his eyes asking for cooperation. "Jill, this is my mother. Margaret Spenser."

"You didn't fire Celia, did you?" Mrs. Spenser turned her back on Jill to glare at her son.

"No, Mother, you know she's coming back after the holidays."

"So this one is only temporary."

Anger flashed in Spenser's eyes and Jill saw his jaw clench. He was upset with his mother's rudeness. But Jill didn't care about the woman's dismissal of her. What did upset her was conflict. She avoided it at all costs.

Besides, something more important was clicking in her brain. She needed a few minutes to think the plan through, but it could work. Her pulse quickened at the possibility.

After all, who would think of looking for her in the sub-urbs?

"Hey, Min, I have an idea." She stood and took the child's hand. "While your dad and grandma talk, let's go fix the Christmas tree."

Mindy scrunched up her nose. "What's wrong with it?"

"You don't know?" Jill reared her head back in mock surprise. "I'll have to show you."

Margaret Spenser turned to them, a strange mixture of surprise and approval in her gaze.

"What about dinner?" Spenser asked.

"We'll have to reheat the casserole, anyway." Jill threw her pseudo employer a smug look as she ushered Mindy toward the family room. This unexpected charade was go-ing to cost him...and maybe save her butt. She had to ad-mit, though, she had little grounds to feel indignant after all the bamboozling she'd already done.

Spenser's low voice faded as they moved into the family room. As soon as Mindy got within several feet of the tree, she frowned. "What's wrong with our Christmas tree?"

Placing her hands on her hips, Jill asked, "Who deco-rated the top?"

Mindy grinned. "Daddy."

"Just what I thought." Jill shook her head at the sterile assortment of blue ornaments. "Not very imaginative, is it?"

The little girl's eyes narrowed as if she didn't understand, and then they widened and she shrugged.

"We'll fix it," Jill said, pulling up a chair, plucking off two balls and handing them to Mindy. "Pass me one of those paper dolls."

Mindy studied the string of doll cutouts. Her hand hov-ered over one for a few seconds and then she chose an angel with long auburn hair and a crooked golden halo.

Jill accepted the cutout and studied it for a moment. "You know what, Mindy? I think you picked out my favorite one. What do you say we put it on the very top?"

Jill angled back to get another look at the tree. It was perfectly shaped, pointy on top, the bottom branches lush and dense, its strong pine scent hugging the room. The fire crackled behind her and she turned, looking for Mindy's answer.

Eyes shining with the reflection of the multicolored tree lights, the child nodded and Jill suddenly got a funny feeling in her stomach. Swallowing hard, she turned to the tree and surveyed the top for the perfect spot. She knew why she was feeling a little sappy. This was the first tree she'd ever decorated, and for whatever reason, it was making her sentimental.

Which made her angry. She had enough trouble on her plate without thinking about the past. Playing the could've/should've game wasn't going to get her anywhere. Staying smart would.

Stretching up on her toes, she tried to snag the branch at the very top but it was an inch out of her reach.

Unexpected pressure at her lower back made her jump, and then Spenser's low rumbling voice brushed her ear.

"Let me help you with that," he said, his hand pressed gently against her waist, steadying her, making her a little dizzy.

She glanced over her shoulder at him, but he was too close and his jaw grazed her temple, sending an unexpected shiver down her nape. Immediately she turned back toward the tree. "Where's your mother?"

"On her way home. Are you trying to reach this one?" He stretched to lower the top branch, his body warming the side of her arm, her right hip and other areas that had no business heating up. How was she supposed to think when he was so close?

She haphazardly hung the paper doll and stepped aside, shrugging away from his touch. He released the branch and the auburn-haired angel sprang to the very top of the tree. It teetered for a moment, and everyone's hands shot up to intercept the fall. But after swaying for a couple of seconds, the angel with the crooked halo smiled down at them, secure in her spot at the top.

Spenser grinned at her. Jill cleared her throat, and stepped farther back. "I guess Mindy had better get to her dinner."

"And you?"

She made a face. "You were right about the cab companies. There's a waiting list, and by the time they get to me, I'm afraid the mall will be closed."

"My offer to drive you still stands. Besides, I owe you." He cast a pointed yet private glance at Mindy, who stood entranced by the tree. "Thanks for before."

"No problem," she said, dusting her hands together. "Now, if you don't mind, I'd like to see my room."

He inclined his head toward her as if he hadn't heard correctly. "Your room?"

"The job includes room and board, doesn't it?" She smiled, but when he only stared back, speechless, she said, "The housekeeping job?"

SPENSER PACED the length of his study, rubbing the back of his neck. Up above, directly overhead on the second floor, he heard Jill bump against something and he stopped to stare at the ceiling.

He was out of his damn mind. This woman was a stranger. A nut. A Santa impersonator. For all he knew, a Santa mugger. What was he doing letting her move in?

Even if it was for only a week. He had Christmas to worry about, his nosy, domineering mother to fend off. And above all, he had Mindy to consider.

Jill quieted down and he resumed his pacing. Of course, Mindy was a large reason he'd decided to let Jill stay for now. It had been a long time since his daughter had been so animated. He'd even had trouble getting her to bed tonight. She was so excited about having Santa's helper stay with her, she'd made a list of all the kids she was going to call.

Jill hadn't been crazy about that idea. In fact, she'd been downright squeamish about it, which made him uneasy. As soon as she came downstairs, they were going to have a talk. And he was going to get some answers.

The bottom stair squeaked and alerted him of her approach. Something else to include with the leaky basement valve, the loose deck boards and all the other things that required fixing on his never-ending list. Real life wasn't all it was cracked up to be. No wonder his wife left.

He pushed open his study door. "I'm in here," he called to Jill, and she rounded the corner, her expression tentative, the rest of her swallowed up by his navy blue robe.

Once again he was amazed by how young she looked and the sudden sickening thought struck that she could be a runaway.

"Thanks for this," she said, plucking at the folds of the blue velour. "I'm keeping the T-shirt for a while, if you don't mind, but this is warmer."

"How old are you?"

Her eyes widened in surprise, and then she squinted at him, her expression an unholy blend of indignation and annoyance. "Why?"

"Because if you're a runaway, that makes me an accomplice."

"A runaway?" In seconds, her expression slid from irritation to disbelief to gleeful amusement. "A runaway?" she repeated, her laughter filling the room.

He liked the sound of it. Maybe too much. She was definitely young. The carefree, bawdy way she belted out her laughter was a dead giveaway. He folded his arms across his chest. "So, how old are you?"

"Uh, twenty-four."

"Want to try again?"

She glared at him. "Okay...twenty-eight."

His arms slipped from their hold and fell to his sides. "Twenty-eight?"

"Listen, Buster, my birthday isn't for two more weeks and I'm staying twenty-eight until the last possible second."

He shook his head. He believed her. She was far too defensive to be lying. "I'm surprised."

Her glower approached the deadly zone. And then she blinked. "Wait a minute. You thought I was a runaway...as in, underage." Her grin stretched to heaven. "I like that."

He laughed. "Twenty-eight is a far cry from ancient. Why lie about your age?"

"Those skin-care commercials."

He lifted an eyebrow.

"You know...like the one for the moisturizer for skin over twenty-five? I get crazy every time I hear one of those ads." She shuddered and started pacing where he'd left off.

"I see." He didn't. He still thought she was a nut. "And you have a driver's license for me to look at?"

She stopped and slid him a wary sidelong look before resuming her restless pacing. "Oh, sure. When I get back to the mall and get my things."

The dismissive wave of her hand put him on edge. "That

wasn't a suggestion,'' he said firmly, and she stopped again. "I'd like references, as well.''

"References?''

"You have a problem with that?''

She hesitated. "No. Why would I?'' she asked, lifting her chin. "Except this isn't a real job, so I don't see why—''

"You're staying in my house. And I don't know a damn thing about you.''

Her shoulders moved up and down, and then she hugged herself as if warding off a sudden chill. "I understand.''

"So, will references be a problem?'' He watched uncertainty cross her face.

"Can they be from out of state?''

"Don't you live here?'' he asked, and when she nodded, he prompted, "and work here?''

"I don't want you calling my boss.''

Uneasiness crawled up the back of his neck. "Why not?''

"You'll laugh.''

"Try me.''

She scrunched up her face and massaged her left temple, clearly trying to weigh her options. Tension radiated from her like heat from a sunlamp, and he didn't know how hard he'd press if she hedged. She hardly looked like a threat standing there in his robe. While the navy velour hit him at the knees, it skimmed the tops of her ankles, and the sleeves gulped her hands.

She looked a lot younger than twenty-eight, yet there was a guarded edginess to her that a person normally acquired with age and a few hard knocks. Watching her continue to massage her temple, he felt his insides soften.

And then he noticed she was left-handed. Which should

have held no importance, except that his ex-wife had been left-handed, too. And she'd walked out on him. And Mindy.

"The mall is closed now," he said. "I'll take you to pick up your things tomorrow as soon as it opens. You can show me identification then. Those references you can give me now."

Her shoulders sagging, she lowered her hand to clasp the other. "He wants to marry me."

"Who?" The single word came out loud, sharp. She'd taken him by surprise.

"My boss, Maury," she said, her wary gaze following him as he pulled out his desk chair and sat down. "But he doesn't love me," she added hastily. "It's not like I'm leaving him at the altar or anything like that."

This time he massaged *his* temple. Suddenly it throbbed like the devil. "This ought to be good. Go on."

"You don't believe me?" Her hands flew to her hips and the robe slipped down her shoulder. It was bare. Smooth. Silky-looking.

He dragged his gaze back to her indignant, flushed face. "Go on. I'll let you know."

"You don't think someone would want to marry me, do you?"

He stared for a moment, then laughed. "That never crossed my mind."

She yanked the robe back up her shoulder and tossed her hair. Lamplight shimmered off her coppery curls. "I've had plenty of proposals, well, three anyway. That's a lot considering I've never lived in one place for more than a year. Except here, of course. But Maury only wants to marry me so he can save a few bucks on his taxes."

"Charming guy."

She laughed. "Well, he thinks he is. But I guess I wouldn't mind being married to him...*if* I ever thought I'd get married." She frowned. "Well, maybe not." She paused, obviously giving the matter considerable thought. "I'd get married for love or nothing. Except I'm not getting married, so it's a moot point."

The throbbing at his temple did not subside. "Are you trying to distract me, or are you always like this?"

"Like what?"

"So damn chatty."

Her gaze narrowed menacingly. "You're the one who wanted answers."

"I'm still waiting."

She folded her arms across her chest. The robe gaped. He looked away. "I told you. Maury is trying to get me to marry him before the end of the year. I won't do it."

"Let me get this straight." Experimentally, he turned back toward her. Only a small wedge of skin was exposed. He should have felt relief. Shifting restlessly, he said, "This guy wants to marry you for a tax benefit and instead of just saying no, you're taking off?"

Her eyes widened on him as if he'd sprouted an extra nose. "Well, of course. Wouldn't you?"

Although she made no sense, he somehow believed she thought she'd found the most sensible solution. She looked far too incredulous to be faking it.

"No. I wouldn't." And he hadn't run from his responsibilities. He'd given up flying instead.

"Then you don't understand. Maury and I already went through this last year. And the year before. He knows I won't marry him."

This was getting better. "So, instead of confronting your problems, you just take off."

She turned away, a flash of anger darkening her face and robbing her of youth. "Sometimes it's simpler that way."

"Yeah." He snorted his impatience. Apparently his wife had felt the same way.

"I mean, it's really no big deal. I don't have family here. And Christmas was never a major holiday for us, anyway. I'd just as soon get away from all the fanfare."

How did she do it? he wondered, watching her shrug slim shoulders and cast quick unsure glances at him. How could she look so blasted vulnerable while admitting how irresponsible she was? And how in the hell was she making him feel sorry for her?

He huffed out a sigh of exasperation as he rose from his chair and rounded the desk to her. She straightened, startled by his sudden move, but before she could slip away, he hooked a finger under her chin and lifted her face, forcing her to look squarely at him. "Are you telling me the truth?"

"Yes." Her eyes fastened on his.

"That's all there is to the story?"

She blinked. "Yes."

He believed her. Maybe because he wanted to, maybe because he was a fool. "Don't mess with me, Jill. I have Mindy to think about."

"I know." Her eyes softened and her lips curved slightly. Warm breath brushed his chin.

Spenser let her go and put some distance between them. He hadn't even thought about a woman's company in the past year. He didn't want to start now. "We'll swing by the mall and pick up your things tomorrow. In the meantime, I've set out a spare toothbrush in the guest bathroom, along with a few other items I thought you might need."

Stuffing her hands in her pockets, she hunched her shoulders forward. "Thank you."

"No problem."

"Noah?"

He frowned. Generally, he hated being called by his given name, but coming from her it sounded different...almost like an aphrodisiac...

He mentally shook his head. This was crazy. Maybe it wasn't a good idea to let her stay. "It's Spenser."

"Okay...Spenser...I...uh..." She looked down at her toes. "I'm not used to having to depend on anyone else. If I seem at all ungrateful—" She broke off, and slowly shrugging her shoulders, she looked up at him. "Thanks."

He was seeing another side of her, one he guessed she wasn't keen on exposing. But this softer, less guarded person was reassuring to him. Maybe she wasn't a nutcase as he'd originally suspected.

The corner of his mouth turned up, partly in relief. "Why don't you get some sleep? Tomorrow we'll worry about finding you something to wear to the mall."

"Oh, that's okay." She smiled brightly. "I'll just wear the Santa suit."

6

JILL WASN'T SURE how serious Spenser was about her doing the housekeeping thing. And since she didn't know exactly what a housekeeper was supposed to do, the next day she waited until she figured Mindy was dressed and had already eaten before she made her way downstairs.

Cooking might be among her list of chores, and that was a problem. Anything over and above a grilled-cheese sandwich and warmed-up canned soup was beyond her ability. And although she was fairly certain keeping the kitchen clean would be another one of her disdainful duties, not cooking would take care of that.

An awful lot of banging was coming from the kitchen as she tiptoed down the hall. She stopped just short of entering. Thinking seriously about turning around and heading back upstairs, she shifted from one stockinged foot to the other.

"Hey, Jill. I've been waiting for you *forever*."

Mindy's high-pitched whine, coming from the family room, rose above the clanging pots. All noise ceased for several long seconds.

Jill cleared her throat as Mindy skipped across the room toward her, then said, "I hope you didn't hold up breakfast for me."

Mindy giggled. "Of course not. We eat at seven-thirty every morning. It's good for our—" she wrinkled her nose and looked toward the ceiling "—our something systems."

Jill laughed. "Who told you that, your grandmother?"

"No, my daddy."

Spenser appeared at the kitchen door and gave Jill a dry look. His shirtsleeves were pushed up to his elbows and small puffs of soapsuds clung to his tanned forearms. He looked oddly appealing and something fluttered deep in her stomach. She exhaled deeply. Stupid, really, that she would have this reaction. Soapsuds? Sheesh.

And then with a surge of relief, she understood. Soapsuds meant the kitchen was already clean. No mystery there.

"Good morning," she said and continued confidently toward him...and the kitchen.

He stepped aside to let her by. "Mindy, go finish doing your lesson plan. I'll be in to check it in a minute."

"This is supposed to be my vacation." Mindy pulled a long face, but as soon as her father lifted an eyebrow, she turned and scampered off toward the family room.

"You old meanie," Jill said, scanning the counter for the coffeepot. She spotted it...empty...sitting in the sink.

His gaze followed hers. "We get up earlier than noon around here."

"It's not noon yet." She frowned. "Is it?"

He gave her a long look before yanking a pot off the dish rack and rubbing it vigorously with a towel. "Close enough."

"Well, I'm not much of a morning person," she said, yawning, and turned to search the counter for a jar of instant caffeine.

The crack split the air about the same time she felt the sting hit her behind. She jumped, then turned to lean against the counter for support before glaring incredulously at Spenser.

Looking somewhat surprised himself, he snapped the

towel in the air again, this time without a target. "Did that wake you up?"

"I can't believe you did that."

"I could show you again."

Her butt pressed carefully against the counter, she inched down the length of it away from him. "You don't want to play rough with me. I'll win."

He let out a short bark of laughter. "Think so?"

"How about a small wager?"

"You don't have any money."

"Oh, yeah." A frown knit her eyebrows together, then she smiled. "It doesn't have to be money."

"What did you have in mind?" After drying his hands, he tugged down his shirtsleeves. His fingers were long, lean, mesmerizing.

A totally inappropriate thought flittered through her head and shocked the living daylights out of her. "I uh, never mind. When did you want to head for the mall?" she asked, even though she was already having second thoughts about returning to the mall so soon. It had occurred to her last night that putting another day between her and the goons might be more prudent. Especially since she wasn't in any rush now.

"After I check Mindy's work."

She nodded. "About the housekeeping stuff," she said, looking cautiously around the clean kitchen. "What did you want me to do?"

"Check out the freezer." He opened a drawer and sifted through some pencils until he found one that was sharp. "Figure out what we're having for dinner."

"I usually check the Yellow Pages for that."

Slowly, he looked up at her, one side of his mouth lifting. "I bet you do."

"What did you mean by that?"

"One question. Can you cook?"

Normally she wasn't defensive about her lack of culinary knowledge. But she didn't like his smug attitude. "Give me an example."

One dark eyebrow lifted in amusement, his gaze taking in the T-shirt she wore, before he started for the door. "I've put a couple of sweatshirts on the table in the upstairs hall for you until you get your things."

"I thought you wanted to know if I can cook?"

"You already answered."

"I can scramble eggs."

"So can Mindy."

"I didn't ask to be your housekeeper."

Spenser stopped. He didn't turn around right away. He stretched his neck to one side, then the other, and when he finally faced her, she noticed how tired he looked.

"Look, I'll drop you at the mall. Don't worry about my mother. She loves Christmas and all the pageantry." He smiled briefly. "It'll take her a while to figure out you're gone."

Jill picked up the towel he'd thrown on the counter and folded it in thirds, carefully avoiding his eyes. "I'd like to stay. I just don't know what I'm supposed to do."

"Well, keeping Mindy entertained would be a big help for one thing."

"I could do that."

"I'd better warn you. She wants to bake Christmas cookies."

"Oops. Maybe I can teach her the fine art of bakery hopping?"

He half smiled. "Good luck."

"That's what I thought." She leaned a hip against the counter and pursed her lips. "Well, making cookies can't be too hard. It might even be fun. You have a recipe, right?''

He nodded. ''Cookie cutters, rolling pin, sprinkles, the works.''

That sounded complicated. ''Okay, we'll get started right after Mindy is done with her work.''

''We have to go to the mall yet,'' he reminded her.

''Don't you have to go to work or something?''

''No. I work out of my study.''

''But I thought you fly planes.''

The hard set of his jaw made it clear her curiosity was unwelcome before he said, ''By the way, your references checked out.''

''You called, huh?''

''This morning. The Meekers in Cincinnati say hi and they wish you'd come back. And the Greens in Dallas said your job is still waiting for you.''

She smiled at hearing the Meeker name, and a wave of wistful longing washed over her. The older couple had been almost like parents to her. Certainly more than her own father had been. She suddenly missed them.

''Odd thing was that no one I talked to understood why you left,'' he said, curiosity lacing his tone. Not that she was going to tell him anything.

''Well, now that you're satisfied I'm not some psychotic serial killer, there really isn't any hurry to go to the mall and get my driver's license, is there?'' she asked casually.

Apparently not casually enough. He narrowed his eyes. ''I thought you'd be anxious to get your things.''

''I don't really have that much there.''

''Why do I have this feeling you haven't told me everything?''

''I have. Honest.'' She shook out the towel and refolded it. ''It's just that Maury's men—'' She stopped and blinked at his thunderous look. "You know, his friends, may still be keeping an eye out for me and I'd rather they think I already split town."

"Are you really that big a wimp?"

"Me?" The word came out a sputter. "Look, buddy, I grew up on more army bases than you can name, with a drill-sergeant father and a bully for a brother. I learned how to fight the same time I learned how to read. The last thing I had the luxury of being was a wimp."

Silence filled the space between them and she realized that she'd just spilled more about herself than she'd intended. Not that her childhood was a guarded secret, but still...

"I'm not a wimp," she said and folded her arms across her chest.

"So you were a tomboy." Spenser smiled and his gaze roamed her face...her shoulders...her hips. "You grew out of it quite nicely."

Jill squashed the reflexive desire to touch her hair, to moisten her lips. She kept her arms rigidly folded. "Thank you."

She wanted her things, she decided suddenly. She wanted to wear clothes that fit. She wanted to dab on the little makeup she normally wore. She wanted to look nice. But was it worth the risk?

It had taken her a long time to get to sleep last night. She'd replayed her last day with Maury over and over again in her head. She was still coming up blank, if not uneasy.

"Listen, maybe you could lend me a few bucks and I can pick up some things at the corner store. That'll save us a trip to the mall for now and I'll pay you back when I do get my stuff."

Spenser stared at her for a long time without speaking. Finally, he said, "I'll give you an advance on your salary."

"A salary? I don't expect you to pay me."

"This may be convenient for you, but it helps me out, too." He lowered his voice so that she had to step forward to hear him. "It frees up my time to get the last-minute holiday stuff done. This is only Mindy's second Christmas without her mother and it's got to be perfect. I can't afford to have anything ruin it for her. Do you understand?"

A downpour of memories for which Jill wasn't prepared deluged her with the force of Niagara Falls. No Christmas tree. No stocking. No presents. No friends.

No mother.

Where had all that come from? She didn't want the reminders. She didn't want Mindy to have those same memories ten years from now. "I do," she said.

He nodded, his gaze burning a path to hers. "So, Santa, tell me I have nothing to worry about."

She swallowed. "Not a thing."

WHO KNEW one small bag could hold so much flour? Jill looked at Mindy who was blissfully sprinkling green sugar on small perfectly cutout little trees. Flour clung to the tip of her nose and smudged her rosy cheeks. It dusted her pretty red dress and dotted her arms and legs.

Jill started to laugh, which stirred up some of the white stuff, making her sneeze. The reaction sent white clouds into the air, and when Mindy looked up, she started laughing, too.

They'd have to clean this all up before Spenser got home, but in the meantime, Jill simply wasn't going to worry about the mess. Flour or sugar covered nearly every inch of spare countertop, and smudges of butter and frosting smeared cheeks and refrigerator doors alike.

"I didn't know making cookies could be so much fun, did you?" Mindy pressed a small red mint into the top of the Christmas-tree cookie, then grinned up at Jill. "I made a cake once with my grandma but it was kinda boring."

"Really?" Jill smothered a laugh as she pictured Margaret Spenser covered in flour. Somehow, the image wouldn't gel. "What kind do you want to make next? Gingerbread men?"

"We're making more?"

"Sure." She picked up the last sack of flour. It was still half-full. "Why not?"

Mindy wiped her cheek with the back of her wrist, leaving more flour than she removed. "Who's going to eat all of these?"

She glanced around the kitchen and frowned. At least seven dozen candy-cane cookies sat piled on two plates on the butcher-block island. Another four dozen Christmas trees had been crammed into a Snoopy cookie jar, and three more dozen had yet to be lifted from their baking sheets. Dozens more Christmas wreaths and stars and some shapes not too easily identifiable were stacked in every available space.

"Well, maybe we shouldn't make any more," Jill said, her gaze coming to rest on the Spenser-family cookbook. It was at least four generations old and Spenser had explained how it had been passed down from the women in his family.

Thinking about it again got Jill a little choked up. Some day that book would belong to Mindy and then later to Mindy's daughter. And their names would be added to the list on the first page just like the other Spenser women. They in turn would communicate with the next generation through this book.

Jill didn't know why this particular tradition got to her the way it did. There was nothing comparably time-honored in her family. Not that she had any use for this kind of

sentimentality. Mementos only slowed you down. Trave
light and fast, that was her motto.

Besides, all she had to remember her mother by was a
silver locket.

Her gaze drew helplessly down the yellowed page, the
notes carefully written in the margins. "Maybe we can jus
make the gingerbread men then stop. What do you say
Mindy?"

The little girl bit into a Christmas tree and grinned.

"How many of those have you had?" Jill asked, and
Mindy held up four fingers. "Don't eat any more and don'
tell your father."

"Don't tell me what?"

Spenser's voice made it to the kitchen a second before
he did. By the time Jill looked up, he'd crossed the threshold, his stunned gaze taking in the destruction.

His eyes met hers. They weren't happy ones. "I didn'
know there was more snow in the forecast," he said dryly

Mindy giggled, but she looked a little worried as she
glanced around the kitchen as if seeing it for the first time
"That's not snow. It's flour. Have a cookie, Daddy."

His gaze stayed on Jill for almost a minute. "I'll wai
until after dinner. How many have you had?" he asked, his
attention transferring to his daughter.

She exchanged quick glances with Jill.

"She had four," Jill admitted, and when his expression
tightened, she added, "Very small ones."

His stern gaze took in his daughter's smudged dress, the
mounds of flour on the tiled floor, the endless stacks of
cookies. There were no small ones. They were all large
monstrous cookies. More than ten families could eat. "Why
don't you go get cleaned up, Min," he said. It wasn't a
question.

She smoothed out her dress, then shook out the skirt

Flour filtered through the air. Drawing in her lower lip, she reluctantly raised her eyes to her father's. "We have to make the gingerbread men yet."

"We'll do that another day," Jill said quickly, feeling the tension, and started carrying bowls and measuring cups to the sink.

Mindy's wary gaze bounced from hers to Spenser's. When he didn't say anything, she licked her fingers, then scampered off the stool. She did a little hop and jump as if she had extra energy to burn.

Jill cringed. She knew a sugar high when she saw one.

"Take your bath now, Mindy," he called after her as she skipped down the hall. "I'll bring your clothes in a minute."

"Oh, don't hang around on my account," Jill said and bent down to pick up some measuring spoons off the floor. The brown grouting was now white. She wondered how she'd get *that* out. "Go with Mindy. I'll clean up."

"You're damn right you will." He stared at her in disbelief. "What in the hell were you doing here?"

"You wanted us to make cookies."

"You didn't have to demolish the kitchen."

She dumped the spoons and two mixing bowls into the sink and spun around to face him. "You know what your problem is?"

One dark eyebrow raised and an annoying glimmer of amusement flickered in his hazel eyes. "I wasn't aware I had one." His lips curved in a wry, humorless smile. "Present company excepted, of course."

That did it. As he himself had admitted, she was helping him out as much as he was helping her. Annoyed, Jill folded her arms across her chest. And dislodged a clump of flour that had been clinging to her shirt. It puffed into the air and in her face, the white powder settling on her eyelashes and nose. She blinked, coughed.

Spenser's expression didn't give an inch, although she could tell he wanted to laugh. His eyes had turned that interesting shade of green they often did when he was amused, and his lips pursed slightly as though he might be trying to control them.

She dragged her gaze away from his distracting mouth. "Your problem is that you're too uptight."

Both eyebrows shot up in surprise. He blinked and the amazement in his face was gone, replaced by irritation. "You know me for all of twenty-four hours, and you come to this expert conclusion?"

She rolled her eyes toward the ceiling, and frowned. How did flour and sprinkles get all the way up there? Before he noticed them, too, she unfolded her arms and got busy gathering up wooden spoons and cookie cutters. "It doesn't take a genius to see where you got it."

He tried to step out of her way but a gob of butter landed on one shiny black shoe. He stared at it a moment, then skewered her with a dark look.

"Sorry about that." She ripped a paper towel off the roll and handed it to him.

His eyes locked in a stubborn hold with hers, he grabbed the towel, then dabbed at his shoe. "I'm going to regret this, but what were you saying?"

She didn't answer right away. She was too mesmerized by the meticulous way he removed every hint of smudge from the black leather. "This is exactly what I'm talking about," she said finally.

"What?" He glanced up.

"You're just like your mother."

"My mother?" He snorted. "You're crazy."

"Maybe, but at least I don't spend my life straightening pictures."

"No doubt you're too busy cleaning up after yourself."

Her lips curved in a satisfied grin and she lounged against the counter, one finger tracing a lazy design on the flour-covered top. "I expected you to say something like that."

"You trade in your Santa suit for a couch, or something?" Standing, he scowled. "Look, Dr. Jill, get this place cleaned up so we can start dinner. We eat at—"

"I know," she said, cutting in. "Precisely six." Her grin widened.

He muttered something under his breath she couldn't hear. Aloud, he said, "You're one nervy lady."

Shaking his head, he stood there, looking so spit and polished in his gray slacks and navy blue shirt, his disdainful gaze roaming her splattered clothes, the yellow cookie dough caked around her nails, that it made her teeth hurt.

"I know," she said, and flicked a handful of flour at him.

7

SPENSER DUCKED, but it was too late. The white powder burst through the air and splattered his navy shirt, gripping the worsted wool like butter clinging to bread.

"You *are* crazy. Certifiable." He swept a hand over his left shoulder, sending the flour airborne before it settled on his slacks. He was too stunned to think of anything else to say. He hadn't expected this little stunt. Not even from her. "A damn nutcase."

"Oops. Didn't I mention that on my job app?" She dusted her hands together. "Well, I feel much better." Grinning, she added, "I have to admit, you're taking this quite well."

"Think so?" He looked up from inspecting the mess she'd made of his clothes, and their gazes collided.

Her eyes briefly widened with a flash of misgiving, before she shuttered them and lifted a flippant shoulder. "You really aren't that bad," she said. "Implying that you're a picture-straightener was probably overstating things. Still, you can't be so...so uptight with children. You have to give them room for creativity."

He nodded, pretending to give her words some consideration. "So, now you're an expert on child rearing," he said, and moved around the corner of the island closer to her.

Her gaze flicked lower and she seemed to be gauging the distance between them. A suspicious gleam entered her eyes and she shifted from one foot to the other. "I don't have to be an expert. I was a child once."

"Once?" he asked, and inched closer.

Prudently, she stepped back. When he made another move, she tried to dash for the door. But he reached across the island and caught her wrist, stopping her cold.

"Okay, I'm sorry. That was childish." She flexed her hand back, but his grip remained firm. "You made your point."

"I haven't even started."

She pulled back, using the island as leverage between them. "Now who's being childish?"

"Isn't that what you wanted?" He sidestepped to the right, but she scooted to her right, too, and rounded the next corner, effectively keeping the block of wood between them.

"I just wanted you to loosen up. Mindy's a kid. She shouldn't have to worry that you'll criticize her for making a small mess."

Her comment stung. It stirred old memories. "Are you a product of that kind of upbringing?" he asked. "I can see it worked wonders for teaching you responsibility."

Trying to wiggle her hand away from his hold, she said, "At least I'm not too uptight to enjoy life."

"No, you just run from it."

He'd never seen her really angry before, but she was now. She even quit struggling. She straightened, so that she could look him in the eye, and he had to lean forward to accommodate her.

"I have never run from anything in my life," she said, glaring at him through glittering slits.

"What about this Maury fellow?"

"That's different."

"Famous last words."

"We weren't talking about me, anyway."

She was so absorbed with being defensive that she hadn't noticed he'd slipped around the island. When she suddenly did, she jerked her hand out of his grasp. But he caught her again, this time his arm hooking around her waist, until her chest pressed against his.

She tilted her head back to look at him, her breathing hard and uneven. A light blush stained her cheeks and her eyes still flared with temper. "Well, Mr. Straight-and-Narrow, now that you've got me, what are you going to do with me?"

She knew the answer to that question as well as he did. He saw it in the way she moistened her lips, the way uncertainty shadowed her face.

He felt it as anticipation slammed his heart against his chest.

"Chicken," she whispered, and his lips came down hard.

Her startled gasp told him that he'd surprised her, too. Yet her lips were firm against his and it took little effort to get her to open to him.

She tasted of sugar and cookie dough and her own intoxicating blend of imp and siren.

He touched her hair, and realized how much he'd wanted to do that. The discovery unnerved him, and he started to pull away from the silky texture, but a curl spiraled around his little finger as if coaxing him to stay.

He deepened the kiss, and Jill moaned softly.

Their tongues touched, danced, mated. He had to stop soon. It was going to be up to him to end this kiss. He had Mindy to think about.

Mindy. He'd almost forgotten that his daughter was just down the hall, that she could walk in on them at any moment. He took one final taste and was about to break away, when Jill angled her head slightly back until their lips lost contact.

"So you aren't a chicken," she whispered.

"Pretty straight, though," he said, starting to grin. "Not too narrow."

She squinted in confusion, and then as comprehension dawned, her eyes widened and she started to laugh. "I can't believe you said that."

"Yeah, me, too." He let his arms fall away from her as he stepped aside and rubbed the back of his neck. Automatically, his glance swung toward the empty doorway.

"I hear water running in the tub," she said as if reading his mind. "She didn't see anything."

As soon as the words left her mouth, she turned away and started picking things up off the counter again.

"Jill?"

Keeping her back to him, she carried a load of utensils to the sink. "I know it didn't mean anything."

"That's not what I was going to say."

"I should have this cleaned up by the time Mindy is finished with her bath. I have an idea for dinner."

"We need to talk about this."

By the speedy way she moved from one chore to the next, it was clear Jill had no intention of discussing anything. And, frankly, he was inclined to let the matter slide, too. But she was going to be here for better than a week and he didn't want tension between them.

"Jill?"

"I thought maybe we'd have mini pizzas for dinner. I make them on English-muffin halves. We have all the ingredients. You can even have veggies on yours."

"That's right. I forgot." He paused, and she stopped moving long enough to slide him a sidelong glance. "You don't deal with problems. You like to hide your head in the sand.''

She turned to face him and he could tell by her expression that he'd hit a sour note. ''I wasn't aware kissing was a problem.''

''It doesn't have to be,'' he agreed.

She sighed. ''So why are you making it one? Can't we just forget it?''

''Can you?''

He hated to admit how much satisfaction it gave him to see her so disconcerted. But when her hand fluttered nervously to her throat and her tongue slipped out to moisten her lips, he felt a deep sense of vindication for his own reaction to their kiss.

Abstinence had made him hungry and he couldn't recall ever feeling so totally consumed by such fleeting intimacy. Maybe he was just out of practice. He'd been single for a little over a year now, living like a monk, and before that he'd been married for what seemed like a lifetime. And even during the long rocky years while the relationship had floundered, he'd never forsaken his vows.

''Okay, I admit it was a mistake,'' she said abruptly, jolting him back to the present.

''You misunderstand me. I simply don't want you to think I was taking advantage of you.''

''Of me?'' She laughed. ''No one takes advantage of me.''

''So, you think you're that tough, huh?'' He doubted it.

''Not tough. Smart.'' Her forehead creased in thought. ''But yeah, tough, too.''

He smiled. ''Smart enough not to let it happen again?''

''If that's the smart thing to do.''

That wasn't an answer. Dammit. His body struggled against common sense. Strung as tight as he was, it was a wonder he could think at all. "You're the smart one here. Is it?"

Of course it was. So why was he pushing? This wasn't like him. *This* wasn't smart. This was foreplay. And he knew it.

A slight flush pinkened her cheeks and she twisted the hem of her T-shirt until the fabric pulled tautly against her breasts. Her nipples beaded and pushed at the thin cotton.

Pleased as he was to see that she wasn't as blasé as she pretended, his body hummed with an excitement he could ill afford. Mindy was only steps away. Of course he hadn't taken her clothes to her yet. And knowing his daughter, she'd sit in the tub and holler for him until he did. That would buy him time…

Jill released her shirt. "I think we need to cool it."

She was right. Besides, this was totally unlike him. So why was he still picturing Jill stretched out naked, on her back, on the center of the butcher-block island, in the middle of all that flour? He shook his head. Celibacy was making a damn fool out of him.

Wrapping an arm across her chest, she drew a hand up and down her opposite arm. She threw him short cautious glances, making him wonder how much his expression was giving his thoughts away.

He cleared his throat. "You're right. This would never work."

"No." She shook her head, glanced toward the kitchen door, then frowned at him. "Why?"

"Why wouldn't it work?"

"Yeah."

"It's not personal, if that's what you mean."

"Never mind," she said, turning toward the sink and reaching for the liquid detergent.

He massaged the tension at the back of his neck. This

was the damnedest conversation he'd ever had. Most women he knew wanted to talk everything to death. He had to wring everything out of this one. "Jill?"

"You'd better go see to Mindy," she said without looking at him.

"I will." He huffed out his exasperation. "Dammit. I've made you uncomfortable."

"Oh, no." She spun around then. "Not at all."

He wasn't convinced. "Something is bothering you."

She shrugged one shoulder and turned back to filling the sink with sudsy water. "Not really."

"Jill, you're driving me crazy."

"Okay." She turned off the water, and bracing both hands on the rim of the sink, she leaned forward, head bent, and took a deep breath. "I was wondering…I mean, I agree that we shouldn't be…" Without looking at him, she took another breath and he felt lower than a worm. He *had* made her uncomfortable.

She straightened and turned to face him. "I think we should kiss one more time." She blinked. "Just for closure, you understand."

His jaw slackened, and his next breath somehow got trapped in his chest. Her nipples had beaded again. He tried not to look.

"Daddy?" From down the hall, Mindy's shrill voice pierced the silence that had stretched between them. "Where's my clothes? I'm freezing."

Spenser smiled. "Guess I'll have to take a rain check."

SHE WAS NEVER going to be able to look at a sack of flour the same way again, Jill decided as she finished storing the supplies from yesterday's baking marathon. Or a cookie, either. They would both forever remind her of Spenser. And that kiss.

After shoving the last bowl into the cupboard, she stood back to inspect the kitchen. Immediately, she focused on the butcher-block island where Spenser had cornered her, and she sighed at the wave of warm memories that swept her. Although she'd been kissing boys since she was fourteen, Jill was certain she'd never been kissed like *that* before.

Her scalp tingled just thinking about it and a swarm of pesky little goose bumps tightened the skin on her arms and legs.

This was ridiculous. She rubbed her arms and marched in place until she felt normal again. She didn't have much time to plan Mindy's spur-of-the-moment party, as it was, and here she was standing in the kitchen all goo-goo-eyed over someone who hadn't even given her...or the kiss...a second thought.

Which was really for the best. She'd pretty much decided yesterday morning that her time in Michigan was up. When she did leave in the next week or so, it was going to be for good. Maury would understand. He wouldn't be too ticked that she didn't give the travel agency any notice.

Thinking about Maury gave her that uneasy feeling again. She tried to push it aside as she stacked the packages of cookies, then settled on a stool and started to make out her grocery list for the party tomorrow. But it was a short, uncomplicated list since the purpose of the party was to get rid of the cookies, and her mind kept wandering back to Maury and the cash deposit she'd made for the agency, as if it had some significance. She just didn't know what that was.

The idea to call Maury had occurred to her. She wouldn't have to tell him she was still in town. He would assume otherwise. Maybe he would even explain the reason for all the cloak-and-dagger antics. Maybe they'd even have a good laugh over it.

Or maybe the rumors about him were true. And maybe he'd start looking for her again.

That notion sent a shiver down her spine, and when she heard the front door open and close, she knew that Mindy had returned from the neighbor's house. Jill was glad to have the distraction of the active seven-year-old.

As if on cue, Mindy appeared at the kitchen door, her nose red, her face tear-stained. She sniffled loudly and hiccuped.

Jill slid off the stool and rushed to meet her. "What's the matter?"

"I hate Karen and Chris and Jo."

"Oh, sweetie, I'm sure you don't hate anyone." She dropped to one knee and slipped an arm around the girl's thin shoulders. "Why don't you tell me what's wrong?"

Mindy rubbed one eye, her mouth pursed in a pout. "I do so hate them. They're ugly."

Jill hid a smile. "You hate them because they're ugly? I thought you were inviting them to your party?"

"They aren't coming. Nobody's coming."

Frowning, Jill stood. She took Mindy's hand and led her to the small dinette in the breakfast nook off the kitchen. After she sat on one of the chairs, she lifted Mindy onto her lap. Outside the bay window, she noticed two of the neighborhood boys laughing and pointing at the house. Carefully, she angled herself away from the window so Mindy couldn't see them.

The little girl snuggled deeper into Jill's embrace and when Jill brought her arms tighter around the child, a warm fuzzy feeling she'd never experienced before settled in her chest.

"Tell me what happened, sweetie," she coaxed softly.

"They don't believe me. Chris said you can't be Santa's helper. He said you're a fake."

Jill briefly closed her eyes. This was her fault. "Maybe they're just teasing you. When they come to the party and I'm in my Santa suit, they'll have to believe you."

Mindy shook her head, misery darkening her green eyes. "Chris said the suit doesn't matter. He said you're only the real thing if you can go down the chimney."

Jill's gaze narrowed, her blood pressure rising a notch. "Who is this little weasel?"

Mindy's eyes widened. "A what?"

"Oh...uh, who's Chris?"

"He lives on the other side of the Kramers. He's not my friend, but I invited him to the party, anyway." She shrugged her sagging shoulders. "I don't have many friends."

Something swelled deep inside Jill and threatened to cut off her air supply. Memories rushed over her again. Memories she'd thought she'd buried long ago, and for a moment she was that same scared kid being dragged from one army base to the next...without many friends to say goodbye to.

She gave Mindy a quick hug. "We're just going to have to prove that I'm not a fake and he'll have to eat his words instead of our delicious cookies, won't he?"

Mindy nodded uncertainly, then frowned. "How are we going to do that?"

"Well..." Jill mentally flipped through a quick assortment of ideas in her head. And then her mind blanked, leaving her with the obvious and most unwelcome solution. "I guess I go down the chimney."

Mindy straightened so that her gaze met Jill's, her eyes a vivid color, lit with excitement and hope. "Can you do that?"

Oh, hell. "Of course. I *am* Santa's helper, aren't I?"

"That's what I told them," Mindy said, sliding off Jill's lap. Although how the child's feet touched the floor was a mystery to Jill. There had to be at least a foot of clouds between her tennis shoes and the tile. "Will you d-do it now?" Mindy asked, her enthusiasm causing her to stutter.

Any small hope Jill had of wiggling out of this mess evaporated. She glanced out at the crystal-blue sky. Even bad weather couldn't be an excuse to throw in the towel. Maybe she'd just stand around the roof for a while. The kids would eventually get tired or cold and disappear. She smiled at Mindy. "You bet."

The girl's chin lifted. "He's going to be sorry he teased me."

"I hope so," Jill muttered, darting a look at the clock, then standing. Spenser was due home in an hour. She didn't particularly want to have to explain to him what she was doing on the roof. "I'll go get my suit on," she said, and scratched her neck just thinking about the itchy red velvet.

"I'll go tell Chris," Mindy said, heading for the door, a smug gleam in her eyes.

"Don't leave the yard," Jill called to her as the girl scampered out of the kitchen. "And wear your coat."

Mindy hollered something over her shoulder about the little boy having to eat crowbars. Jill didn't correct her but chuckled all the way upstairs. It wasn't that funny and she vaguely considered that mild hysteria might be setting in. She wasn't particularly fond of heights, had no idea how she was going to get up on the roof in the first place and had less of a notion how she would get down the blasted chimney if push came to shove.

Mushrooming doubt shadowed her as she quickly changed into the Santa suit, pulled on the clunky boots and limped her way downstairs. She stopped at the fireplace in the family room and poked her head inside. Narrow. Very narrow. She straightened and stared down at her artificially rounded belly. Maybe a little less padding was in order. But then of course she wouldn't look the part.

Sighing, she made her way out the back door and into the garage. A ladder lay on its side against the rear wall. A sudden appearance on the roof would be far more dramatic, she decided, and dragged the ladder to the backyard and leaned it against the house.

As she made the awkward climb, she heard laughter and excited chatter coming from the front yard and any thoughts of backing out of the deal quickly dissolved.

When she arrived at the top, she inched her way around to the front of the house, clinging to the chimney, thankful that the roof wasn't too steep an incline.

Several squeals from below caused her to lose her footing once, and her heart nearly leaped out of her chest. But she grasped the abrasive brick tighter, the cold seeping through her gloves and sleeves.

She managed a feeble wave and quick glance at the children, their wide gazes glued to her, and then looked down the sooty tunnel and took a deep calming breath. She could do this, she told herself. She had no choice. Mindy was counting on her.

8

SPENSER HEARD the sirens taper off just as he turned onto his street. Relief wasn't immediate, however. His heart still pounded wildly and his palms had grown so moist he had trouble holding on to the wheel.

It sounded like a two-alarm fire. He knew from experience, he thought grimly as his thoughts drew back to another time when he'd sat on the runway in a disabled plane, lights flashing, passengers screaming.

He pushed the unpleasant memory from his mind. There had already been a couple of false alarms in the neighborhood since the holiday season started, something to do with excess cooking setting off smoke detectors. Mindy was fine. Jill was fine. He was overreacting.

As he veered around the last curve in the road, he strained to see at which address the fire trucks had stopped.

His heart somersaulted.

Two walls of red metal obscured the view of his house. One of the trucks was parked haphazardly across his driveway. The other one took up half the street as two firefighters pulled off a ladder and hurried across his front lawn.

He didn't see any smoke coming from the house, and his gaze darted to the clusters of people standing outside watching the commotion. He spotted Mindy right away, her hands pressed to her flushed cheeks, wide frightened eyes trained on the roof, and leaning against his neighbor, Rose

Manning. His pulse did a frenzied jig before slipping into lower gear.

He threw the car into park, and climbed out while taking deep, steadying breaths.

Jill.

He froze. Why wasn't she with Mindy? His frantic gaze combed the crowd of spectators. Not a redhead in the bunch. Hurrying toward Mindy, he told himself to calm down. There was probably a good reason for Jill's absence. No one looked overly concerned. In fact, the Browns from three houses down were laughing. So were the Masons.

Mrs. Peyton, from directly next door, stood with her hand on her hip, shaking her head. Nothing went on in the neighborhood that she didn't know about, and she generally overreacted to everything. Right now, he was relieved to see that she looked more disapproving than worried.

As soon as Mindy spotted him, she broke away from Rose Manning and hurled herself at him. He scooped her up in his arms, his body humming with both tension and relief.

"Are you okay, baby?" He reared his head back trying to get a look at her face. But her small arms clung fiercely to his neck, her face buried, pressed to his throat, the telltale feel of her tears on his skin. "Mindy, are you all right?"

"She's fine, Noah. There's no fire." Rose rushed over to reassure him. There was a chilly bite in the air and the woman shivered in her lightweight sweater.

"Jill?"

"You mean Santa?" A smile tugged at Rose's thin pale lips as her blue gaze drifted toward the roof of his house. "She'll be okay, too."

"I'm sorry, Daddy." Mindy finally pulled back and hiccuped.

"Why, baby? What happened?"

"I'm sorry Jill got stuck on the roof. It's my fault."

"She's on the roof?" His voice rose and the few people who hadn't been eyeing him were now.

"In the ch-chimney."

"What?"

Mindy shook her head, sniffled and buried her face again.

Rose laid a hand on his arm. "I'm freezing. I'm going to duck inside and put on a pot of coffee. Want some?"

Spenser smiled at this neighbor. She'd been a good friend to him, especially since Susan had left. A divorcée with two kids of her own, Rose had helped him out with Mindy more times than he could count. But he suspected she wanted more than he could give right now.

He shook his head. "I'd better get to the bottom of this."

Nodding, she patted Mindy on the back. "Santa will be okay, sweetheart. Don't you worry. Call me," she said, glancing at Spenser before dashing across the snow-covered lawn to her front door.

Heaving a weary sigh, Spenser gave Mindy another hug, then set her on the ground, his eyes trained on the firefighters climbing the ladder to the roof. He grabbed Mindy's hand and headed for the unsmiling man in uniform standing near the garage.

By the time he got there, the spectators broke out into applause and he looked up to see a fireman escorting Jill down the ladder. At least he figured it was Jill. She wore the red Santa suit, half covered with soot, and she was missing one boot.

He stood back and waited for her to hit the ground, and when he realized she looked okay, irritation overshadowed relief. He couldn't wait to hear what this was about.

"Do you know what a damn-fool thing that was to do?" the younger, shorter fireman who'd brought her down said as soon as they reached the ground. He pulled off his helmet and shook his head, his expression thunderous. "You caused an awful lot of trouble for nothing, kid."

Jill growled and pulled down the grimy fake beard to let it hang limply from around her neck. A smoggy cloud of soot rose from the whiskers and she sneezed. The action caused her already loose cap to tumble forward, and Spenser caught it. Immediately, a mass of coppery curls sprung to life.

"You're a woman?" The fireman's jaw slackened, and he looked at his partner, who seemed equally surprised.

"No, I'm an elf." She sneezed again and briefly covered her face with her hand, leaving a fresh streak of grubby ash across her cheek. The rest of her face fared no better, with the exception of her jaw and chin where the beard had protected the area.

She wrinkled her nose in an effort to avoid another sneeze and her annoyed expression dissolved. Looking suitably contrite, she said, "A very sorry elf. You're right. That was a stupid thing to do."

The man tucked his helmet under his arm and smoothed back his disheveled blond hair, his sudden interest as plain as the pretty pink staining Jill's cheeks. He smiled at her. "No problem. Any bumps or bruises?" He picked up her gloved hand as if inspecting it.

Oh brother. Spenser snorted loudly. No one paid him any attention.

"How about we go inside and you get out of that getup?" the young man said, still smiling, his teeth white against a remarkably tanned face. "We can check for any...damage."

Jill opened her mouth to answer but nothing came out. Her gaze swept the sea of interested onlookers. She cringed as her eyes met Spenser's, and more color surged to her face.

He was tempted to let her fend for herself. She certainly deserved to get out of this mess on her own, but glancing at the eager young fireman gave Spenser new perspective.

He stepped forward. "I think the only damage may be to the young lady's ego," he said in a low voice. "Thank you, gentlemen. I'll take it from here."

One of the men nodded and started back toward the truck.

The younger one turned to frown at him. "You her father?"

Mindy had been quiet and still until now. She giggled. "He's *my* daddy. Not Jill's."

Spenser squashed the curse on the tip of his tongue. He wasn't *that* old.

"I'm their housekeeper," Jill said, her amused gaze finding Spenser's. A grin broke out across her face and, freeing her hand from the man's grasp, she reached over to ruffle Mindy's hair. "And Santa's helper."

Most of their audience had started to disband, but she casually glanced around at the handful of youngsters who lingered. Leaning back, she patted her padded belly. "But I'd better go on a diet or I won't be helping Santa this Christmas."

Then she threw in a loud ho-ho-ho, which made Mindy beam.

The young fireman's eyebrows rose slightly and he gave Spenser a befuddled look as if asking if this was some kind of joke.

A smile tugged at Spenser's mouth. Good. He hoped the guy thought she was a complete fruitcake. His smile faded. Hell, she *was* a fruitcake.

"Can we go inside now?" he asked with his last shred of patience. "It's got to be twenty degrees out here."

Jill shivered and briefly hugged herself. "Feels even

colder." She extended her hand to the young man, a tentative smile playing about her lips. "Again, thanks. Sorry to be so much trouble."

"Brad." The fireman squeezed her hand. "My name's Brad." His gaze flicked to Spenser and back again. "Listen, how about if I call you later to see how you're doing?"

She blinked. "Well..." Her voice trailed off, her gaze straying toward Spenser.

"Come on, Mindy. Let's go get something warm to drink." Spenser tugged at his daughter's hand. She came willingly. Too willingly.

The little turkey normally argued about everything. Now that he wanted an excuse to hang around, the kid finally decided to listen.

Spenser muttered to himself as he stomped the snow free of his shoes, then led Mindy through the front door and into the kitchen. Sugar and cinnamon from yesterday's baking lingered in the air. Packages of cookies, from colorfully decorated Christmas trees to red-and-white candy canes, were stacked up on the normally tidy counter.

"Can we have hot chocolate?" Mindy asked.

"It's too close to dinner," Spenser said, and stuck the teakettle under the faucet. From the window over the sink, he had a view of the fire trucks but not of Jill. Or her smitten rescuer.

"I don't think we have any dinner. Can't I have chocolate? Please." The last word ended on a whiny note, and when Spenser turned to give her *the look,* he caught her inching toward a package of green-iced Christmas wreaths.

"Touch that, young lady, and you'll be in more trouble than Jill."

Mindy's dark head whipped around and her startled green eyes met his. "Jill can't be in trouble."

"You want to bet?" He gave her a dry look as he carried the kettle to the stove and turned on the burner.

"Don't be mad at her, Daddy." She hunched her tiny shoulders and shook her head. "You can't be."

She looked so small and forlorn standing there that it gave Spenser pause.

And then he got irritated all over again. Jill had put his daughter in the position of having to defend the indefensible. What she'd done was totally irresponsible, dangerous and a damn bad example for all the neighborhood kids.

She was lucky it hadn't snowed since yesterday, that the wind had blown the majority of the stuff off the roof. Even so, the incline of the shingles alone made her actions dangerous. Especially with those ridiculously large boots.

His heart started to pound again, as the possible, albeit avoided, consequences sunk in. And when he realized he was reacting far too much to a woman he barely knew, his anger doubled.

Yeah, she was in trouble, all right.

"Hi."

The object of his annoyance stood in the doorway, her hair in wild disarray from the wind, and her face flushed, presumably from the wind and cold...or maybe from her admirer. Flecks of snow dotted her smutty Santa suit.

She'd removed the remaining boot, and in her pink-stockinged feet, she strolled into the kitchen. From the cabinet to the right of the sink, she removed a mug, and said "Anyone care to join me for some peppermint tea?"

"Mindy, go wash your face and hands," Spenser said, his gaze remaining steadily on Jill.

"But, Daddy, I don't want you—"

"Now isn't the time to argue, Min."

"Oh, I see you already have the water on," Jill said

quickly, and set her mug on the counter. "I'll go clean up, too."

"Not so fast," he said before she made it to the door. "I have one question for you."

She slowed down and cast a wary glance his way. "Only one?"

"Mindy." The stern tone of his voice sent her scurrying for the door, but she gave Jill a hasty smile before padding down the hall.

Jill wasn't in any hurry to acknowledge him. She watched Mindy for a few moments, then when she finally faced him, a guarded look darkened her violet eyes.

He exhaled loudly. "*What* were you thinking?" Shaking his head, he drove a hand through his hair. "Or were you?"

She made a face. Then she made an odd buzzing noise. "Penalty whistle. Two questions. Not one. You forfeit the match."

Unsmiling, Spenser stared at her. "This isn't funny, Jill."

"I made a mistake. I screwed up. Is that what you want to hear me say?" She pressed her hands to her smudged cheeks, covering her mouth, and blew into her palms. Then she yanked them away in agitation. "Look, I am sorry. In retrospect, what I did was probably wrong—"

"Probably?" he repeated, interrupting her. "That's precisely what scares the hell out of me. You're like a big kid. Impulsive. Stubborn. Rash. Indulging your little fantasies on a whim. You can't act that way in front of Mindy."

Her face paled. She stared back, her lips parting slightly as though she was on the verge of saying something. Only nothing came out. He saw the movement at her throat as she swallowed convulsively.

"You're right." She drew in her lower lip. "About all

of it. I'll apologize to Mindy before I leave. If you don't mind, though, I'd like to clean up first.''

Wordlessly, Spenser watched her slip out of the kitchen. She'd taken him by surprise. He hadn't expected her to go for good. He'd only wanted her to think about her actions. But maybe it was for the best. He wasn't sure he wanted to leave her alone with Mindy anymore.

He scrubbed at his eyes while exhaling a long cleansing breath. He needed a minute to think.

Mindy's dark head poked around the corner. Her face was blotched the way it often was when she became overly emotional, and her eyes were filled with tears. ''Don't make Jill leave,'' she said. ''I want her to stay.''

''You shouldn't have been listening,'' he said, leaning wearily against the counter. Life was supposed to be getting easier, not more complicated. He'd worked hard to smooth out the vast changes thrown at them in the past year. He'd been making progress. Mindy was starting to come around. She was responding well to him as an authority figure and a friend.

Mindy stomped across the tile floor, and grabbing his hand, she tried to pull him toward the door. ''Tell her she has to stay, Daddy.''

So much of life he couldn't control, so many decisions he made regarding his daughter he made with uncertainty. He couldn't willfully ignore the obvious fact that Jill was a bad influence.

He let Mindy pull him as far as the door, then he stopped. ''I know you don't understand, honey, but sometimes even grown-ups do things that aren't right.''

''I know,'' she said, nodding, her eyes large and round. ''I won't scold you.''

He laughed. ''I'm not talking about me.''

She wrinkled her nose. ''Not Jill,'' she said with solemn confidence. ''She was being the good guy.''

Great. Now she even sounded like Jill. And she'd only been here two days. It was best that she was leaving. So why wasn't he happy about it?

''She did it because my friends laughed at me. Jill tried to go down the chimney for me, Daddy.''

SHE DIDN'T have anything to pack. The Santa suit was pretty much ruined, and Jill wondered if Spenser would begrudge her the use of his T-shirt and sweatpants until tomorrow. He'd looked pretty angry. She wouldn't be surprised if he told her to stuff it.

After washing her face and hands and counting four hives on her chest, she stripped the peach-colored sheets off the brass queen-size bed she'd slept in last night and bundled them in her arms. The least she could do was drop them into the washer before she called a taxi. The thought of leaving bothered her more than the hives did. Spenser might think he had everything under control, but he didn't. He was too busy being Mr. Perfect to realize that his daughter didn't have many friends, that they'd even teased her about not having a mother anymore.

She sighed, and a sharp pain stabbed at her side. She'd really done a number on herself, trying to shimmy down that damn chimney. That little incident would certainly hit the record book as one of the stupidest stunts she'd pulled, and she'd tackled some whoppers in her time.

As she reached the door, someone knocked. She opened it while cradling the sheets in her arms.

Spenser stood there, his broad shoulders spanning the width of the door. He didn't say anything right away. He just stood there staring at her. ''I was wrong,'' he said finally.

"No, you weren't." She shrugged. "I'll be ready to go as soon as I drop these in the washer. And as much as I hate to ask to borrow cab fare..."

He wouldn't let her pass. She took a step forward, but so did he until she was forced to back up or run smack into him. As soon as she cleared the threshold, he followed her in and closed the door.

"This is a little heavy-handed," she said, not knowing quite what to make of his behavior. "Even for you."

"I don't want you skipping out of here before you listen to me."

"I don't feel like another lecture about running from responsibility. Thank you very much."

"Don't worry. You're not going to get one," he said, taking another step toward her.

"Where's Mindy?"

"She's across the street at Rose Manning's house."

"Don't want any witnesses, huh?" she said, joking, except her pulse had picked up speed. He looked different somehow, more formidable.

"Knock it off, Jill, I'm trying to apologize."

"Why? You were right. I was wrong."

He laughed, and although it was a short humorless sound, he looked a little more like the old Spenser. "I wish it were that simple. But the gray area tripped me up."

"Am I going to want to hear this?"

"Put the sheets down," he said, stepping closer still, his eyes meeting hers, dark, dangerous, inflexible.

"I like them right where they are," she said, hiking the heap of soft cotton up under her chin and tripping over an area rug when she tried to move back. She righted herself and stared him down.

"You don't trust me? What do you think I'm going to do?"

"Maybe I don't trust myself," she said, hoping to shock him a little.

He didn't give her the satisfaction. One corner of his mouth lifted and he said, "I like that."

"Hey, Buster, what did you do with the real Noah Spenser?"

This time his laughter was filled with amusement. "What's the matter? Can't handle this one?"

"Give me a break." She hugged the sheets tighter to her chest. "What happened? A few minutes ago I was pond scum."

"Okay, so now I'm pond scum."

"Yeah?" She grinned suddenly. "Why?"

"Mindy told me why you were on the roof. Not that I think you made the wisest choice. But I do appreciate the gesture. And now she's very upset about you leaving."

Jill blinked. Her arms relaxed and a pillowcase toppled to the floor. She hadn't been prepared for the sudden jolt of disappointment. It shouldn't matter that this had to do with Mindy and not his wanting her to stay. But it did, and she wasn't sure where the feeling of dejection came from. She only knew that she didn't want the sappy emotion to stay.

He picked up the pillowcase and tossed it on the bed. "Don't go, Jill."

She sank to the edge of the bed and dumped the rest of the sheets on top of the pillowcase. It didn't surprise her when he sat down, too, just a foot away, his knee nearly touching hers.

"Nothing has changed," he said. "You still need a place to stay and we need some help around here. It's hard for me to watch Mindy all day and work on my design. Especially with her being out of school and all the extra Christmas activities."

He made sense, which proved little comfort to her bruised ego. But it was hard to concentrate on what he was saying and deal with this new and unnerving feeling of neediness.

She stared down at her hands for a moment, then looked up at him as something he'd said sunk in. "What design?"

"It's a small project of mine." Shrugging, he made a dismissive gesture with his hand, and she got the distinct impression she'd treaded upon something he didn't want to discuss. "I'm working on a jet-engine modification."

"A *small* project?" She smiled. "Sounds impressive."

"If it works." He cleared his throat. "Are you going to stay?"

She plucked at the hem of her T-shirt, but he stopped her by covering her hand with his. "I suppose it does make sense," she said slowly, trying to ignore the warmth his casual touch generated.

"Mindy would be very pleased." He smiled as if he'd just played the winning card, and she smiled back faintly because it was better than gritting her teeth in front of him.

Besides, it was easier this way, she told herself. A mutual attraction would complicate things. This one-sided one was bad enough. But, despite her errant feelings, there was good reason for her to stay: to let things with Maury cool down. She could handle her sudden, stupid, single-minded fascination with this man.

She took a deep breath. Again, sharp pain jabbed at a point just below her ribs and she gasped.

"What's the matter?" Spenser's casual touch tightened. "Jill?"

"I'm fine," she said, her free hand automatically going to her sore side.

He frowned in that direction. "You hurt yourself, didn't you?"

"It's probably only a bruise."

His eyebrows rose. "Probably? You need to see a doctor."

"No, I don't," she said quickly. She hated doctors. She'd had her fill of army quacks. "I really don't. I just need..." Words seemed to fail her as her gaze connected with his probing eyes. "I, uh, I need..." She looked away, hoping he didn't see it in her face, the hopeless, raw urgency swelling inside her.

Hooking a finger under her chin, he drew her back to him.

But it wasn't her eyes his gaze touched. It was her mouth.

Right before he lowered his head.

9

SPENSER KEPT the kiss soft and gentle. He realized after he'd acted on his crazy impulse that she might really be hurt and he didn't want to cause her any more pain.

He reluctantly pulled back, but he kept his finger under her chin so she couldn't look away.

Her eyes, wide and questioning, made her appear very young. No wonder the fireman had thought she was Spenser's daughter. In many ways Jill was still young, carefree. He, on the other hand, had a lot of responsibility he couldn't ignore. Sometimes the pressure made him feel a hundred years old.

The reminder was sobering and he dropped his hand. "That wasn't the best time to collect on that rain check. I'm sorry."

"Is that what you were doing?" She lifted her chin and some unidentifiable emotion flickered in her eyes. It could have been disappointment, hurt, maybe even challenge. He didn't understand it, whatever it was.

"I'm not sure what I was doing." He rammed a hand through his hair. "I hope I didn't just discourage you from staying."

An unexpected giggle burst from her lips. She shook her head, setting her beautiful auburn curls in motion around her face. "No, Spenser, you didn't."

He frowned at the giddiness in her voice. Maybe she was

in shock. "We're going to get you to a doctor right now," he said, and started to stand.

Grabbing his hand, she jerked him back down to the bed. "I'm not going anywhere. I'm fine."

"What about your side?"

She lightly pressed a probing hand to her waist. "It's a little sore, but it's just a bruise. Nothing to worry about. Believe me, I know the difference."

"Oh, yeah. I forgot, you were a tomboy." He gave her a wry smile. "Can I see?"

"See what?"

He nudged his chin toward her waist, and concern flashed across her face. "You're hiding something."

"I'm not." She jerked up her T-shirt. She still had the Santa-suit pants on with its voluminous waist and it sagged low, hugging her hips, exposing her navel.

He'd never given much thought to navels before, but there was something inordinately sexy about hers, and his chest tightened in response.

"Where does it hurt?" he asked, his voice coming out in a surprisingly even tone.

"Right here." She grimaced slightly when she pressed two fingers at the indention of her waist.

The flesh was only faintly discolored at this point, but he could tell that it was on its way to a healthy bruise.

"May I?" He put out a hand.

She nodded, and when he gently touched her skin, he heard her sharp intake of breath.

"Sorry," he mumbled, pulling back.

"Oh, it didn't hurt."

His gaze flew to hers. A faint rosiness was seeping into her complexion, and she quickly lowered her lashes.

"I'll tell you what," she said, tugging the shirt back

down and cutting off his view of all that smooth satiny skin. "If it still hurts tomorrow, I'll go to the doctor."

He smiled. "Without an argument?"

"Probably a small one, but that's my best offer."

"I like arguing with Mindy better."

Jill chuckled. "You'd better go get the little munchkin. I'll put these sheets back on the bed."

"Mindy is fine for a few more minutes. I'll help you make up the bed." He slid back toward the center of the mattress and bounced. "Good firm springs," he said, then stood and grabbed the hem of one of the sheets, but she yanked it out of his hand. "What?" he asked.

"Don't worry about—" her gaze wandered across the rumpled sheets, the shiny brass posters "—the bed."

"Two people will make the job easier."

She raised an arm and pointed to the door. "Out."

He reared back. "What are you so touchy about all of a sudden?"

"I'm counting to three."

"Okay, okay. I'm out of here already." He scowled on his way to the door.

But only because he didn't want her to see how relieved he was, to see that he affected her as much as she did him. He bit back a grin as he let himself out, leaving her to stare at the bed...and wonder.

JILL FINISHED putting away the unused paper plates and napkins, and slid a look at Mindy's shining face. She didn't know how Spenser had managed to get all the neighborhood children to come to Mindy's party, or, for that matter, convince their parents that Jill really wasn't some kind of kook. But ten very full and happy little monsters had just left and Mindy looked as if she were in seventh heaven.

"Why don't you go wash your hands and face before

our daddy flips his lid?" Jill suggested, and Mindy giggled.

"He doesn't have a lid. Only pots and pans have lids." Mindy reached for another Christmas tree–shaped sugar cookie.

Jill swiped the plate off the counter in the nick of time. "Oh no you don't. You're going to end up with a tummy ache."

"Jill," Mindy started to whine.

"Save it, kiddo, no more sugar or I'll have to peel you off the ceiling."

"Careful, sweetheart, you're starting to sound like an adult," Spenser said as he carried in a tray of empty milk glasses and set it over the dishwasher.

A small silly thrill shot through Jill at hearing him use the endearment. Although she understood it wasn't *really* an endearment. Not in this case.

"That'll never happen," Jill said, laughing.

"Speaking of aches, how's the side?"

She rolled her eyes toward the ceiling. "No different than the other two times you asked today. Fine."

"How bruised did it get?"

"I'll show you." She grabbed the hem of the gray sweatshirt he'd lent her, and his gaze flew to his daughter.

"Jill told you to go get cleaned up, didn't she?"

Mindy heaved a long-suffering sigh. "Yes." She turned around and stomped out of the kitchen and down the hall.

Jill lounged back against the counter and cocked her head to the side. "What did you think I was going to do? Strip?"

"No telling with you."

"Relax. I filled my quota of impulsive wacko stunts for the year."

"Too bad." His voice had dipped, making him sound

sexier than usual and she gave him a double take, wondering if she'd heard him correctly. He lifted his chin toward her midsection. "Let's see the damage."

Now that Mindy wasn't here to chaperon, Jill didn't feel quite so blasé about pulling up her sweatshirt, even if it was only a couple of inches.

"It's really small," she said, lifting a nonchalant shoulder, then inching the sweatshirt up.

Sympathy shadowed his face. "Ah, Jill, that's not a small bruise." He stepped forward, concern replacing everything else. He trailed a light finger around the affected area. "I don't know that there's anything we can do for this." He frowned up at her. "Is there?"

His gentle touch gave her a small shiver. She promptly let her sweatshirt down and hunched her shoulders forward in a deep slow shrug. "For a bruise? I don't think so."

Helplessness and agitation formed an alliance to darken his expression. He huffed out a sound of exasperation. "Susan knew about all this stuff. Mindy always went to her."

"Your wife?"

"Ex-wife," he said abruptly. He gestured to her clothes. "You must be getting pretty tired of wearing those old things. Let's plan on heading for the mall to pick up your stuff before dinner."

"The mall?" She opened the dishwasher and busied herself with stacking glasses inside. "It's only four days before Christmas. It'll be too crowded. Let's wait."

The silence stretched long enough for curiosity to force her to glance at him. His gaze was narrowed on her.

"You'd rather wear my hand-me-downs?"

"Well, no, but it's not like I have anywhere to go, and besides, I already bought all the cosmetics I need from the corner drugstore."

"You're worrying me again."

She waved a hand. "I'm sure it's safe to go back."

"Safe?" He cringed.

She blinked. "For lack of a better word."

"What did you say your boyfriend's name is again?"

"Maury, and he's *not* my boyfriend."

"Maury what?"

"What is this? Census time already?"

"Jill." His drawl made her name a warning. "Can we go over this again?"

"What's to go over?" She turned away from him and fiddled with the bottom rack of the dishwasher. It always stuck if she jerked it out too far. Now seemed like the perfect time to fix it. At least the exercise would be an excuse not to look at him.

He was making her nervous the way he was angling his head to the side, as if trying to study her every nuance, as if he could see right through her.

When she wouldn't respond, he finally said, "I'm invited to a party this week. I'd like you to go with me."

"A party?" She straightened. "Where?"

"A company I'm consulting for. They're sponsoring my designs and I really feel like I should show up. Besides, it might be fun."

Anticipation sparked and did a tango down her spine. Which surprised her. She wasn't much of a party person, although she normally did okay at them. But this would almost be like a date. With Spenser, she thought, getting all tingly again. She could get dressed up and...

She made a face. "But I don't have anything to wear."

"That's why we have to go to the mall."

"Oh. Well, I'm really not the party type."

"You looked like you were a moment ago," he said, a suspicious gleam entering his eyes. "Does this sudden shift have anything to do with not wanting to go to the mall?"

"No, because I don't have any suitable clothes there anyway."

"We could swing by your apartment."

"No." She all but shouted the word. "Maury may have staked—" She stopped herself and quickly rethought her phrasing. "If I didn't think Maury may still look for me there, I'd be home now, wouldn't I?"

"What did you say this Maury's last name was again?"

She drummed her fingers on the edge of the counter and stared at him. Why was he being so stubborn all of a sudden? Although her boss had had several brushes with the law, it had been a long time ago over minor incidents— hardly front-page news. At least that's what he'd told her. Of course, there were also the rumors about him being tied to the Capello family out of New York, but she knew better. That wasn't true. She hoped.

"It's Montague," she said finally.

Spenser smiled. "As in *Romeo and Juliet?*"

"Believe me, he's no Romeo."

He frowned. "I wonder if that's why the name sounds familiar. Montague, huh?" His gaze drifted out the window, concentration deepening the creases in his forehead.

"He owns a travel agency, for goodness' sake. Unless you use Midas Travel, there's no reason you would know him."

"Hmm." He switched his puzzled gaze to her. "Midas Travel sounds familiar, too."

"I give up." She threw her hands up. "You're making way too much of this. If you want to go to the mall, we'll go."

He gave her a bland look. "Just like that?"

"If that's what it takes to prove to you that my misguided paranoia is the only thing you have to worry about."

Her indifferent manner seemed to mollify him, and he

thoughtfully pursed his lips as he regarded her. She wished she could be so easily placated. Just thinking about going back to the mall and possibly facing those goons gave her the willies.

Of course she was being paranoid. There was no way those guys could still be looking for her. They'd have to figure she was long gone. She and Maury had already gone through this last year. Certainly he didn't think she was still hanging around.

But this time was different, an eerie, nagging voice reminded her. His family was involved. His not-so-conventional family. The ones who rode around in window-tinted limos and made Maury sweat.

Rubbing her clammy hands together, she realized Spenser was still watching her closely. "What sort of party is this? Casual? Dressy?"

"Probably dressy, but not necessarily black-tie."

"I'll have to buy something new. Are there any nice shops close by?"

He arched a suspicious eyebrow. "I'm sure there are plenty of suitable stores at the mall."

Okay, so she was a little transparent. "Sure."

"By the way, I'll spring for the dress."

"You will not."

"This isn't charity. You're doing me a favor by going as my date."

She straightened at hearing the D-word. Of course he was using the term *date* loosely. She knew better than to read too much into it. But it had been a long time since she'd been with anyone she liked as much as Spenser.

Being a good father had never been part of her criteria for judging date material, she'd simply not thought much about that aspect. But she found she really liked that Spenser was so good with Mindy. Even though at times he was a little too rigid for Jill's tastes, he showed genuine concern about his daughter and he admitted when he was wrong.

He'd also expressed concern for Jill. Without a motive or agenda. Just simple, bona fide concern. It had been a long time since anyone had done that. And she discovered she wanted very much to be Spenser's date, if only for a night.

"Jill? Did you hear me?"

His voice penetrated the brief fog she was in and she blinked at him.

"I said I'll drive you to find a dress."

"You don't have to do that. I know you're busy with your work. If you don't mind lending me your car, I'll take care of it."

"I'd prefer to drive you."

"Don't you trust me to come back?" she asked, teasing, but when his expression tightened, she knew she'd struck a nerve. "You don't think I'd run off with your car, do you?"

He massaged the side of his neck. "Of course not. I didn't mean to give you that impression." Pausing, he seemed at a loss for words. Then he said, "I just figured I'd do the last of my Christmas shopping at the same time."

He was lying. Well, maybe not lying but certainly trying to sidestep. Never having been known for her tact, Jill saw no reason to change the status quo. After a moment's deliberation, she asked, "Does this have to do with your wife?"

Slowly, he stuffed his hands into his pockets and glanced toward the doorway. "Little ears sometimes have big radar."

"And I shouldn't be prying, right?"

"No, you shouldn't." A faint smile curved his lips. "But that won't stop you."

She placed a hand over her heart. "I'm offended."

"Does that mean the inquisition is over?"

If he had seemed upset, she probably would have let the subject slide. But he appeared okay with her curiosity. "Not on your life."

"That's what I thought." He heaved a long weary sigh and glanced toward the door again. "I can't say it was a total surprise when she left. I knew she was unhappy. But I hadn't expected to come home to a 'Dear John' note."

Jill's heart thudded. "You mean, you went to work one day, then came home that night and boom?"

"I was on a trip. When I used to fly, I'd be gone for days at a time. I think I'd been gone nearly a week when it happened."

"And Mindy?" she asked softly, sliding a look at the empty doorway. "Where was she?" When her gaze returned to meet his, she was saddened by the pain she saw there. Immediately she regretted bringing up his daughter.

"Susan left her with my mother."

Jill let a colorful word slip before she could censor herself. "That's horrible," she added quickly, in a futile attempt to cover her gaffe. "Did you look for her?"

His expression clouded and he stared at Jill as if she'd lost her mind. "No. She made her choice."

No gray area there. That was clear. Not knowing what to say, she said nothing.

"I wasn't blameless," he added. "I'll never deny that. I cared too much about work for too long."

"That's not a crime."

"Nor is it very responsible."

It was hard to reconcile the picture he painted of himself with the man she knew. The one who put Mindy before anything else. "You're a good father, Spenser."

He half smiled. "I guess you *can* teach an old dog new tricks, huh?"

"Don't be flip about this. I'm serious. I wish I'd had a father who cared half as much about me." Too late, she realized the significance of what she'd said.

"Thanks." He stared thoughtfully at her and there was no mistaking the growing curiosity in his expression. She braced herself for an unwelcome question, but he merely added, "I really mean that. Thanks."

"Good. Because I meant it, too." She smiled, wondering where the sudden and uncharacteristic attack of shyness was coming from.

She still had more questions, like why he was no longer flying. But now that she'd just set herself up by getting personal, she wasn't about to open that floodgate.

"Now," he said, flexing his shoulders. "Let's talk about something more pleasant."

"I agree."

"Like what you're making for dinner?"

"Dinner?" Her smile faded abruptly. "I don't suppose you mean reservations?"

He chuckled. "Not a bad idea. After that little shindig you threw today, you deserve a night out."

"The kids were fun," she said, mildly surprised that she meant it. "But I'm beat and if you want takeout for dinner, I won't argue."

"Let's go out, instead."

She wasn't overly keen on that idea. Of course, she didn't have to be dressed for a place like a kid's pizza parlor. Nor would she expect to run into Maury at a place like that. "What's Mindy's favorite? Chuck E Cheese's?"

"That's not what I had in mind."

Cocking her head to the side, she frowned quizzically. "What then?"

"Mindy's had a full day. She'll be sacked out soon."

"And?" Her pulse tumbled into high gear.

"I was thinking just the two of us, a bottle of wine, some pasta. Light on the garlic." He studied her face, his gaze briefly snagging on her lips. "Maybe no garlic. How does that sound?"

"Dangerous."

Slowly, he grinned, a great deal of satisfaction radiating from the small action.

She groaned. Why couldn't her mouth wait for instructions from her brain? It was a simple process. Most people understood that. Jill wished she did. "I mean, Mindy can't go to sleep too early. You know she goes to bed at precisely the same time every night and if we disrupt her routine—" She stopped at the look of surprised amusement on his face, and she realized what she was saying. "Oh, no, you've got me doing it, too."

He laughed. "Don't look so worried. A little order in your life won't kill you."

"I don't like order. It scares me." Not quite sure where that assertion came from, she stared back at his thoughtful expression. He was analyzing her. She didn't like it. "Besides, Mindy still needs to have dinner, too, and we can't leave her alone."

"I have a couple of baby-sitters I can call. And as far as dinner, with all the junk she ate today, some tomato soup and a salad will be fine for her."

"What do you mean junk? Were those great cookies, or were those great cookies?" she asked. She was proud of herself. Except for the few burned batches, she'd done a remarkable job. Especially considering the closest she usually came to an oven was to stick in a TV dinner.

Although the kids obviously agreed, having gobbled up an astonishing amount, what had really pleased her was

Spenser. He alone had scarfed down at least a dozen cookies since yesterday.

"Some people find modesty becoming," he said, laughing.

"Oh, I can't take credit. It was the Spenser cookbook," she said, surprising herself. She hadn't given the book any conscious thought. But there was something magical about it, she admitted. Something that made her feel warm and included. Which was total nonsense and a little far-fetched, even for her inherent bent toward the absurd.

"I'm glad you like the book. But I think you may have had a little something to do with your success," he said, winking. "You know, we do have some nice wine here. There's fresh pasta in the fridge that wouldn't take us long to whip up. About as long as it would take Mindy to hit the pillow."

"Maybe that isn't such a bad idea." She told herself not to get excited. This was merely a practical suggestion.

He took her hand. "Then maybe I can collect on that rain check."

Jill silently cleared her throat and decided not to point out that he already had. "I think that can be arranged." She congratulated herself for sounding calm, cool, composed. But when her gaze suddenly drew to the butcher-block island, a searing heat wave of memories made her pulse skid out of control.

Spenser looked down at the patterns he was tracing on her hand. "Jill, I hope——"

A yowl came from down the hall, and their gazes collided.

"Mindy," they both said at once.

Spenser dashed to the door first.

Jill followed right behind him.

10

MINDY LAY across her bed, flat on her back, her arms wrapped around her stomach when Spenser entered her room. His gut clenched at the sight of her tearstained face, tightened in agony.

"Baby, what's wrong?" he asked, kneeling beside her. "Does your tummy hurt?"

Struggling to catch her breath, she nodded.

Too many cookies. Briefly, he closed his eyes and chastised himself for his negligence. He knew better. He should have monitored more closely what she'd eaten at the party.

"Do you think maybe you ate too much sugar?" he asked gently as he pressed the back of his hand to her forehead. No fever.

She shook her head. "I didn't have any sugar. Only seven—" She frowned. "Nine cookies."

He sighed. "Does your tummy feel like it did when you had too much cotton candy at the circus that one time?"

Nodding a second time, she struggled to sit up. "It feels a little better now."

Out of the corner of his eye, he saw Jill hovering near the doorway, an anxious expression on her face.

He waved her inside. "A case of overindulgence," he said over his shoulder, and started feeling guilty again. He should have been paying more attention to his daughter and not Jill.

"Hi, sweetie." Jill moved to stand beside the bed and

brushed the hair off Mindy's forehead. "Your tummy may hurt, but your lungs are in good shape." When Mindy frowned in confusion, Jill laughed softly, and said, "That was a good yell. They heard you all the way to the North Pole."

Mindy offered a weak giggle. Then she sniffed and asked, "When are you going to see Santa again?"

"Well..." Jill drew her eyebrows together and stared at the ceiling as if giving the matter serious thought. "I have to work two shifts on Christmas Eve. All his helpers do. That is our busiest night of the year, you know." Mindy nodded solemnly, and Jill grinned. "But I think we have one more meeting before the big night. Why, sweetie?"

"I have something I want you to ask him."

Jill darted Spenser a glance. "Is there something else you want to add to your list?"

"Sort of." Mindy tried to straighten more and grimaced with the effort.

"Let's talk about that later," Spenser said, and urged her to stretch out again. "Christmas Eve isn't for three more nights. You have plenty of time."

"Only three nights?" Jill's face paled.

Spenser tempered a grin. She certainly played her part well. "Yup, only three more nights," he said, returning his attention to Mindy. "And then all the good little boys and girls get a visit from the big man himself."

"Three nights," Jill repeated.

The dread in her voice made him turn toward her again. She looked paler still, almost as if she was going to be ill. "Jill? What's wrong?"

She pressed a hand to her stomach and wrinkled her nose. "I think I overdid it, too. How many cookies did *you* eat, Min?"

Mindy's eyes widened. "Nine." She glanced nervously at Spenser. "And a half."

"I think I beat you."

He squinted in disbelief. "Are you serious?"

"I wouldn't kid about something like this." Jill's pained expression overshadowed her feeble attempt to curve her lips. "I think maybe I'll go lie down, too."

"Good idea," Spenser said, unsmiling, and watched her drag herself slowly to the door. It wasn't that he was unsympathetic, but rather annoyed that she'd been so foolish.

"You be good and stay still, Min," she said, pausing. "We'll play a game of Old Maid later." She cast a quick, apologetic glance at Spenser. "I guess you're on your own for dinner."

He nodded, feeling a little out of sorts himself. Not because he'd eaten too many cookies. He knew better. Obviously, Jill didn't. And that was part of the problem. She didn't want to grow up. Whereas he had no choice. He was a father with responsibilities.

Although you'd never know it, he thought grimly. Because of his preoccupation with Jill lately, he'd been a poor father. Bad enough he was already doing penance for being an absent husband and father, someone who valued his career and love of flying above everything else. He couldn't screw up a second time around.

Canceling dinner was for the best, he told himself, tucking the covers around Mindy. Jill was a distraction he couldn't afford.

IF ONLY she'd gotten a good night's sleep, Jill was certain she could have figured out what to do next. But she'd tossed and turned until dawn and now, a little before noon, she was still as much a basket case as she'd been when she'd lied about eating all those cookies.

She finished trimming the crusts off Mindy's bread and cut the sandwich into perfect little rectangles, just the way the little girl liked them. Staring at the strips of whole wheat, Jill made a face. She'd bet either Mindy's grandmother or Spenser had encouraged this absurd little rectangle fetish. Wielding the knife again, she created a pair of squares and two elongated triangles.

Tilting her head slightly to the side, she stared at her handiwork. Hell, she must be tired. Now she was even challenging poor Mindy's eating habits. She doubted the girl would appreciate this lesson in flexibility.

She sighed. In two nights, it would be Christmas Eve. She felt like Cinderella approaching midnight. Except there was no Prince Charming waiting to sweep her away into a happy ending. She had only herself to rely upon. Her mind started to wander toward Spenser and she ruthlessly stopped it.

She'd been happy here. Too happy. That's why time had gotten away from her.

Christmas Eve was a big night for Maury and his family. The entire Montague clan celebrated together, and she'd decided that would be a good time to clear out her apartment.

Most of the contents were either rented or makeshift pieces of furniture. Nothing she'd miss. But there were a few items to which she'd grown attached. Photos mainly, of people she'd met in the past few years. And the silver locket. The only thing her mother had left her.

And then, of course, there was Christmas Day itself. What a drag that was. She shook her head. She'd forgotten to send her father's present. Although she wasn't sure if he was still in Germany or not. And since she hadn't a clue about her brother's whereabouts, she wasn't worried about his gift.

"What are you mumbling to yourself?" Spenser asked, startling her from behind. After he reached into the refrigerator and withdrew a pitcher of iced tea, he peered over her shoulder at Mindy's sandwich. "She doesn't eat it like that."

"Fine. You want it? I'll make her another one."

"Well, no. I like it the way Min does."

"Of course you do." She wiped her hands briskly on the towel, then carried the plate to the table.

His hand slowed as he reached into the cabinet for a glass, and he frowned at her. "What are you so wound up about? Eat too many cookies again?"

If she'd been restless and edgy before, she was twice as irritable now. He'd been in his office all morning, which had suited her fine. She wished he'd stayed there.

"If you want to keep working, I'll bring you your lunch in your study," she said without looking at him.

"Trying to get rid of me?" Hurt tinged his voice and she stopped her aimless fussing with the stack of paper napkins.

As soon as she looked at him, she knew what was eating at her. She studied the familiar way one side of his mouth quirked when he was puzzled, the way one stubborn lock of dark hair swept his eyebrow. And she knew she wanted to stay. With Spenser. With Mindy. She wanted to be a part of their family. She wanted the impossible.

"I'm not trying to get rid of you. I was just..." What was she supposed to do? Spill her guts? She blew impatiently at a stray curl that caught on her eyelash. "Look, do you want lunch now, or not? This isn't a restaurant."

Spenser grunted. "Excuse me for breathing."

She glared at him for a moment. "Sorry," she mumbled, and took a deep breath as she turned to get Mindy's milk.

"Are you still feeling sick?" he asked, his expression

concerned, making her feel like a bigger jerk for being so grumpy.

"It's Christmas." She waved a hand and nearly sent to the floor the glass of milk she'd just poured. Spenser swept the milk out of her reach. "This whole holiday ho-ho-ho thing. It makes me nuts. I just don't do Christmas well."

"What?" His chortle brimmed with sarcasm. "Don't even try it, Miss Let's-bake-a-thousand-cookies-and-have-a-party-for-a-hundred-kids."

"That was a mistake, and you know it."

"What about the tree? Let's see, how many times have you stripped and redecorated it now? Three?"

"Hey, that wasn't my fault. You're the one who messed it up in the first place."

"How can you mess up decorating a tree?"

She put a hand on her hip. "It was too...orderly."

"And you're the expert?"

"Well, maybe I've never decorated one before," she said, lifting her chin, "but at least I have imagination."

He set Mindy's milk on the table, his gaze glued to Jill. The glass clanged against the lip of the plate, and the liquid sloshed over the rim onto his hand. He ignored it. "You *never* decorated a tree before?"

Her chin lifted a notch higher. "Is that a crime?"

"Why?"

She flipped her hair back over her shoulder and reached for a sponge, intent on wiping down the counter. This discussion was getting personal. She'd rather clean the kitchen.

"Is it against your religious beliefs?" he asked.

"No."

"Were your parents anti–Santa Claus?"

Shaking her head, she moved to the sink and started to

scrub the chrome faucet, concentrating on each small groove.

Silence stretched until he asked, "Are you going to ignore me the rest of the day?"

She jerked a shoulder. It was supposed to be a casual gesture. She probably looked as though she had a twitch. "We moved around a lot."

"Every Christmas?"

"What are you doing, writing a book?"

"Oh, so it's okay for you to take my inventory and compare me to my mother, but I can't make simple conversation?"

"My dad was an army sergeant who had to drag two kids around from one base to another. He didn't give a damn about Christmas or Santa Claus." She pushed away from the sink and looked at him. Pity darkened his eyes.

"Don't do that," she said. "I mean it." She threw the sponge into the sink and opened the lower cabinet in search of a bucket. She was really losing it now. She never did anything so drastic as mop the floor.

"Do what?"

"Feel sorry for me."

"Why would I do that?"

"I know the symptoms." She got on her hands and knees and stuck her head in the deep cabinet.

"Hmm. Nice visual."

She didn't like the way his voice lowered and she backed up to get a look at his face. He was looking at her butt. "Knock it off."

"What?" He laughed. "I'd much rather talk to you face-to-face, but hey." He raised both his hands, palms out. "I'm not complaining."

His ploy worked. She wiggled backward until her head was completely clear of the cabinet. The sweatpants he'd lent her made her rear look hideously large. And at this particular angle, with her shirt hiked up…she shuddered thinking about it.

Jill glanced at the wall clock as she started to get to her feet. "Oh, no, it's two minutes after twelve and Mindy hasn't started eating lunch yet. Better get her in here or she'll need therapy for the rest of her life."

She put a fluttering hand to her throat, pretending to feel faint, and got punished for her corny dramatics by nearly losing her footing.

He grabbed her arm to steady her. "I see. We can't talk about you, but it's okay to take shots at me."

She regained her balance and tried to shake free of his hold, but he only tightened his fingers and drew her closer. She splayed one hand across his chest. His heart beat against her palm steady and strong and she forgot that she'd meant to push him away.

Hesitantly, she raised her gaze. It made it as far as his mouth, where small tension lines bracketed his lips. He'd missed a tiny speck of whiskers near his jaw when he'd shaved earlier. His nostrils flared slightly.

Finally, she looked into his eyes. They told her plainly that he wanted her.

She cleared her throat and shifted back a few inches. "I don't like talking about myself."

A slow smile curved his lips.

"Okay, that's no news flash," she admitted. "But that doesn't mean I should be taking shots at you. I'm sorry."

"I'm not being nosy, and I certainly don't pity you. You look like you grew up okay to me. I just want to know what makes you tick."

"Why?" she asked, starting to pull away. They were too close to be having this conversation. She was feeling suddenly and inexplicably needy.

He let her go, and disappointment spiraled through her.

"Because I care about you," he said, his tone so casual it took her a moment to process his words. "But we'll have plenty of time to talk later. Why don't you call Mindy to the table? I'll phone Rose across the street. She's offered to watch Min while we go shopping. I'll send the little cookie monster over after she's finished eating."

Plenty of time? That wasn't going to happen. She had to get out of town. She had to…

Her thoughts came to an abrupt halt. "Shopping?" she asked, and instantly remembered. "The party."

"It's tomorrow night."

"I forgot."

"You sound hesitant."

"Why don't you take Rose?" she asked the moment the impulsive idea struck. "I'm sure she already has a dress, and I could watch Mindy, and…I hear she's divorced."

"Well, I suppose I could," he said slowly, and the sudden burst of indignation she felt must have shown in her face because he promptly grinned. "But I want to take *you*." He touched the tip of her nose and a disgusting and unexpected heat flash warmed her cheeks.

"Besides," he said, his smile broadening. "I'm kind of curious."

Don't set yourself up, she warned herself, then kicking herself, instantly asked, "About what?"

His gaze made a leisurely trip down her body. "What you really look like."

She squinted, unsure what he meant. And then she knew. The sweatpants. Her big butt. Well, it wasn't that big. That was the point. But he wouldn't know that, it only looked that way because of the…

She squinted harder. Oh, he was a sly one. But once again his ploy had worked, she admitted as her vanity slowly caved in.

With a haughty lift of her chin, she turned toward the

door. "Mindy, lunch," she called out. Then over her shoulder she said, "I'll be ready in ten minutes."

JILL SPOTTED Mary Ellen Sawyer as soon as the older woman came through the boutique door, and all Jill could think about was the line in *Casablanca* about gin joints. Why did the woman have to stroll into this particular shop?

Immediately, Jill did an about-face, presenting her back to her favorite customer. Mary Ellen loved going on cruises and she booked them through Maury's agency often. Unfortunately, Mary Ellen loved to talk, too. To anyone who would listen...that included Maury.

Damn.

This was a relatively small town. It shouldn't surprise her to see someone she knew. But that's why she'd avoided the mall. This shop was a neighborhood boutique. She thought she'd be safe here. As slim as the possibility was, she didn't need any Jill-sightings getting back to her boss.

While keeping one eye on the woman's progress via a three-way mirror, she tried to get Spenser's attention. He'd stationed himself on a chair near the dressing room and had his nose stuck in an aeronautics magazine.

"Spenser."

He didn't look up.

"Noah," she called more urgently.

He lowered the periodical and frowned. "Yeah?"

"I can't find a dress. Let's get out of here."

"I liked the blue one. Try it on."

"Wrong size."

"What about the one in your hand?"

She jammed the shimmering green silk back on the rack. "Can we go?"

His gaze shifted from side to side. "Why are we whispering?"

"I'll tell you outside."

She watched Spenser sweep a suspicious gaze around the small boutique. It was fairly crowded with Christmas shoppers, and a large decorated tree sitting in the middle of the store provided a welcome, albeit temporary, obstacle between them and Mary Ellen.

But he wasn't in any hurry, it seemed, and Jill felt her patience slip.

The hell with him. She hiked up her too-big sweatpants, then started to inch toward the door, darting glances up and down the aisle. Mary Ellen was short, and Jill had lost sight of the woman's blue-gray hair behind the cashmere coats a couple of seconds ago.

But since it was a clear shot to the exit, Jill figured she could make it outside without incident. She took one final look around and straightened confidently before sauntering toward the door.

"I thought that was you." Mary Ellen popped out from behind a rack of beaded sweaters, her twinkling blue eyes taking in Jill's odd appearance. "Hard to miss that beautiful head of hair. But I thought you were out of town."

"Hi, Mary Ellen." Jill hiked up her pants again, increasingly conscious of her bag-lady appearance. "I *am* out of town. I mean, Maury thinks I'm out of town."

Although the older woman smiled, she managed to look mildly disapproving. "I know. Does that mean the wedding is off?"

Jill made a face. From her peripheral vision, she noted that Spenser had finally decided to join her. Except that he hung back, although not out of earshot, she noticed.

"The wedding was never on. Maury was just being…Maury. You know how he is…" Jill shrugged, offering a conspiratory smile. "A little impulsive at times."

Spenser coughed.

Jill didn't give him the satisfaction of so much as a passing glance. She concentrated on her customer, who nodded wryly. "So, I'm sure you understand, Mary Ellen," she continued, while staring meaningfully at the woman, "why I don't want him to know I'm still here."

"My lips are sealed. I'm sure you have your reasons. You know you're my favorite agent, Jill, always taking such good care of all my travel arrangements. You remind me so much of my granddaughter. Such a sweet-tempered child you are."

Spenser coughed again, and this time Jill sent him a quick glare. Grinning broadly, he winked.

"Thanks, Mary Ellen," she said, refocusing her attention and patting the woman's arm. "Don't stay out in the cold too long. You know how your elbow acts up."

The woman nodded and sighed. "Such a dear. Maybe you should reconsider marrying Maury. He's not such a bad sort and he'd take good care of you."

Jill eyed the door. It was definitely time to leave. This was not the time or place to assert her independence. Although the thought of anyone taking care of her made her want to gag.

Mary Ellen obviously noticed her edginess and waved her on. "Run along. But if you change your mind, I expect an invitation to the wedding."

"You can go ahead and fill up your calendar," Jill said, laughing on her way to the door.

"Too bad about all the family. But I guess it can't be helped."

Jill stopped and turned, her eyes briefly meeting Spenser's, a chill seeping into her joints. "What family?"

"Maury's family." Mary Ellen shrugged. "Dozens of them hanging around the agency. I assumed they're all in town for the wedding."

Jill blanched. Here for the wedding? She didn't think so. And she sure wouldn't bet her life on it.

11

SPENSER WRESTLED with his left cuff link for almost five minutes before he admitted to himself that he was nervous. He finally snapped the little sucker in place and took a deep, fortifying breath.

If he could skip the party tonight, he would. But attending was more for business than social reasons, and he'd been working on his design for too long to let any opportunity slip by. Enough important people in the aeronautics community would be there to make his appearance worthwhile. After he collected enough names and business cards, he'd be out of there.

Then he'd be free to tackle his real problem.

Jill.

She'd been restless since her encounter with the older woman yesterday. She'd even been uncharacteristically absentminded, pouring Mindy three different glasses of milk for dinner, then sticking the mashed potatoes in the refrigerator instead of the microwave.

When he'd asked her what the problem was, she'd breezily changed the subject. But he knew the wheels were turning in her head. It was scary how well he was getting to know her, despite her efforts to maintain that invisible barrier between them.

He straightened his tie, then glanced at his bedside digital clock. He was early. He wondered how long he'd have to wait for Jill.

He didn't have to wonder long. When he got downstairs, he saw her sitting in the semidark family room, near the fire, staring at the lighted Christmas tree.

The different-colored lights shimmered off the emerald green silk dress she wore and her hair was a halo of fire. She almost didn't look real, sitting there, transfixed by the beauty of the tree and looking so beautiful herself that his eyes stung. He blinked. They really did sting. And then he noticed the room was a little smoky.

"You were roasting marshmallows again, weren't you?" he asked, smiling.

Startled, she jumped, automatically dabbing a finger at the corner of her mouth, searching for evidence. "How could you tell?"

"You dropped some into the fire again."

"Only one." She gazed into the air above her, then waved a hand. "Oops. I'd better get out of here. I don't want my new dress to smell like smoke."

Rising from the wingback chair, she carefully smoothed the silk around her thighs, the fabric clinging to curves he hadn't known she had. The dress ended several inches above her knees and if he'd realized what incredibly shapely legs she had, no way would he have lent her those ugly sweatpants for so long.

His mouth went dry, and he felt as eager as a teenage boy noticing the opposite sex for the first time.

She moved toward him but stopped halfway across the room. "Did I thank you for the dress?" she asked, looking anxiously down at the garment and back to him. Although the neck was high and the sleeves long, a diamond cutout framed creamy cleavage. "It's a perfect fit."

Perfect fit? Sheer perfection was more like it. He couldn't take his eyes off her.

She folded her arms across her chest. "It doesn't look right, does it?"

"What?" He frowned, and realized he'd been staring. "You look beautiful...stunning, in fact."

Her shoulders moved self-consciously. "I guess you already dropped Mindy off at your mom's."

He nodded. "An hour ago. She's probably inventoried all of the presents under her grandmother's tree by now."

She grinned. "That's my girl."

"You're both incorrigible."

"Yeah, but you love us, anyway..." Her voice trailed off, the last word barely discernible. Eyes widening, she was clearly flustered over what she'd said.

"You're right," he said, presenting an arm and trying to ward off the smile tugging at his lips. She'd only been using a figure of speech. They both knew that. But that she'd been so disconcerted by the innocent remark spoke volumes to him.

He let the smile take over his face. He'd decided last night that he wanted her to stay. But he had questions. And by her reaction, he'd just gotten one of his answers.

She was no more immune to him than he was to her.

JILL WALKED SLOWLY across the marble foyer, her arm tucked firmly in Spenser's. The black heels he'd picked out for her were a little higher than she normally wore, when she wore them at all. And the last thing she wanted to do was fall on her behind in front of a hundred people.

At least a hundred. Maybe two.

She inclined her head close to his, and whispered, "I should be really ticked at you. I had no idea there would be this many people here."

He shook his head, and she got a whiff of something

woodsy and distinctly Spenser. "Me, neither. This is the first year I've come to this bash."

"Do you know anyone?"

"Only the most important person here." He disengaged their arms, then slipped his around her shoulder and drew her close.

Taken by surprise, she nearly stepped on his foot. He did a fancy two-step and saved his toe by a fraction. His arm dropped in the process and she gave him a helpless look.

Smiling, he patted her hand, then squeezed it, keeping them joined as they proceeded across the spacious foyer.

Although the moment passed quickly, it seared an imprint in Jill's mind. Something had changed between them. If his words or actions hadn't clued her in, the look in his darkened eyes would have, and she wasn't sure how to handle it. Or if she even wanted to do anything about it. After all, she was leaving tomorrow.

Wasn't she?

Of course she was. She had no choice. What else was she supposed to do about Maury and that whole mess? Yesterday, Mary Ellen had confirmed Jill's worse suspicion. There was far more trouble brewing than a marriage of convenience. She felt it in every bone of her body.

Ironically, having overheard her conversation with the woman, Spenser seemed more relieved. He now knew for sure that Jill was telling the truth about Maury and the ridiculous marriage proposal. Little did he know that appeared to be the least of her current problems.

"Look at that," Spenser said as they entered the main room. Following the direction of his gaze, she saw a huge Christmas tree in the center of the room. Although it was obviously professionally decorated in coordinating blue and silver ornaments and stars, the tree was spectacular and Jill's eyes widened in appreciation.

"Wow, they needed a ladder to reach the top of that sucker." She sized up the tree. It had to stand at least twelve feet, each branch perfectly symmetrical.

He chuckled. "It's really something, all right."

"I like ours better."

He turned to give her a long look and a self-conscious warmth crept into her face. She hadn't meant to say "ours."

"I like ours better, too," he said, squeezing her hand. "You and Mindy have done a good job renovating it."

"I don't know if I like that term," she said, laughing. "We just did a little rearranging."

A waiter stopped to offer them glasses of champagne, which they each accepted. Behind him, someone dressed as Santa handed roses out to the ladies.

"A relative of yours?" Spenser asked as he steered them farther into the room. Against the back wall, a parquet dance floor had been set up where a tuxedo-clad band played.

"Probably," she said absently, eyeing the dancers.

A sudden case of jitters made her hands clammy and she pulled subtly away from Spenser just as he started to direct them toward the buffet table. Apparently, her action wasn't subtle enough. He stopped and gave her an odd look.

"What's wrong?" he asked. "Did you want to dance?"

She shook her head. "Actually, I was hoping you wouldn't ask."

"That makes me feel much better," he said with a wry twist of his mouth.

"Nothing personal. I just don't know how."

"Everyone knows how to at least slow-dance."

"Not this someone." It seemed as though every time she'd been about to go to a high-school dance, her father was packing them up and moving them again.

"It's not hard. I could show you how in a couple of minutes."

"In front of all these people? No, thanks," she said, watching as another couple glided across the floor, arms wrapped intimately around each other. She cast a private glance at Spenser. He was watching them, too, looking incredibly handsome in his navy suit and crisp white shirt. She decided she certainly wouldn't mind if he held her like that. Maybe she could get by with just shuffling her feet. But the gliding stuff was definitely out.

"At home," he said, catching her gaze. "Later, we'll practice in private."

"Good idea." *Right.* She cleared her throat. "Don't they believe in chairs at this party?"

"Over there," he said, nudging his chin toward a far corner, his worried eyes not leaving her. "Do you need to sit down?"

"Not yet."

Tables and chairs were set up, the tables each decorated with elaborate centerpieces consisting of giant white mums, silver mirrored balls and white netting. So far, Jill's feet were doing okay, but she knew exactly where she was going if the too-high heels started to bother her.

When she realized he was still genuinely concerned, she said, "It's the shoes. I'm not used to these heels."

"I didn't think about that." He looked down at the pointy black patent leather, and added, "Sorry."

As his gaze continued to travel up her calves, to her knees and higher still, she straightened uncomfortably. But she couldn't help feeling a little heady over his obvious appreciation. Had anyone else given her the once-over like that, she'd have been tempted to deck him.

"Only a man would buy heels this high, you know," she said to reclaim his attention.

His eyes briefly met hers, and then they flickered away, toward the dance floor. Numerous pairs of beaded and sequined shoes, as equally high as hers, peppered the floor.

"Okay, and a few insane women," she said dryly.

"Never mind. I get your point. You'd have to put me in a straitjacket before I'd wear something like that."

"I bet." She grinned. "Hmm, interesting concept—you, a straitjacket and heels."

"Don't be a smart aleck. If you hadn't dashed out of the store yesterday, you could have picked out your own shoes."

"All right." She waved a hand, anxious to end this conversation. "No more complaints from me."

"That'll be the day."

"Hey. Am I a complainer?"

His lips curved into a smug smile. "Only when you're hungry and cranky, darlin'. Speaking of which..." He spread his hand toward the buffet table.

Before she could deliver a worthy comeback, a barrel-chested man with a white goatee ambled up to them.

"Noah. Noah Spenser." The man extended his blue-veined hand. "Glad you could make it, son."

"Efrem." Spenser nodded as he shook the man's hand. "It's a pleasure. Thank you for having us." Then he stepped to the side to include Jill in the huddle.

He started to introduce them, when the older man enveloped her in a huge bear hug. "Mrs. Spenser, so delighted to finally meet you."

Although he let her go as quickly as he'd embraced her, it took Jill a few seconds to catch her breath, more from surprise than anything else.

"Hold on, Efrem," Spenser said, smiling easily. "I'm still working on the *Mrs.* Spenser part."

She glared at him incredulously and he winked before

returning his attention to the other man. "This is Jill Morgan. Jill, this is Efrem Wadell."

"I sure am sorry. I didn't mean to be rushing things along," Efrem said, grinning and not looking at all contrite. "You'll excuse an old fool his shortcomings, won't you?"

She smiled graciously. Spenser would be dealt with later. "Why, Mr. Wadell, I suspect you're anything but a fool."

Just for the fun of it, she'd laced her voice with a hint of the southern drawl she'd picked up when living in Atlanta for a year. She did a fair imitation of the locals when she was in the mood to put someone on. And from the look of surprise on Spenser's face, he considered her imitation pretty damn good.

Efrem Wadell beamed at her. "You're as charming as you are pretty, my dear. If this old boy here doesn't hurry things along, I'll just have to snap you up myself." Old enough to be her grandfather, he let out a belly laugh that had several people looking in their direction.

Two of the men who'd glanced over clearly recognized Spenser because they wandered over to shake his hand. He promptly introduced her to the pair, then Efrem kept bending her ear. She only half listened, though, while she eavesdropped on the others.

"How close is your design to the production stage?" the tall blond man named Ron asked, and Spenser's smile disappeared.

"I'm not at liberty to discuss that." Spenser sipped his champagne and gazed idly about the room.

She didn't know how well these men knew him, but he didn't fool her for a nanosecond. His jaw clenched and unclenched a couple of times, and behind the casual facade his eyes were both alert and uncomfortable.

"Come on," Ron said, a shrewd gleam in his eye. "We

flew together too long for you to give me the brush-off like this."

"So you know me well enough to know that's all you're getting."

The two men laughed. Spenser barely smiled. Then Ron said, "Okay, Noah, just tell me when you're coming back. Those skies are gettin' mighty lonely without you." Ron gave his companion a friendly swat on the arm. "Hey, Larry," Ron said to the second man, "that sounds like one of your country-and-western songs, huh?"

Larry shook his head, darting Spenser an oddly sympathetic look before frowning at his friend. "Better switch to cola, pal. Free bubbly ain't gonna sound so good tomorrow morning."

Ron ignored him, and took another gulp of his champagne. "So, when are you coming back?"

"My flying days are over," Spenser said, grim-faced. "Nothing's changed."

"Lord, Spenser, half of us don't have wives, but we got kids and we still fly."

"So, Jill." Efrem tapped her arm and she jumped, not realizing how blatantly she'd been eavesdropping. "What do you say we take a spin around the floor and leave these fellows to powwow for a while?"

She stared mutely at him for several long seconds, then she smiled. "That's a great idea, Efrem, thank you."

He beamed and put out an arm for her to take.

She patted it. "It was very nice meeting you." And then she swung around, grabbed Spenser's hand and batted her lashes. "I hate to interrupt, but you did promise me this dance."

Spenser's eyebrows knit together. "You want to dance?"

"You promised," she repeated through clenched teeth

and a bright smile. She couldn't stomach the eyelash batting again. Either he got it or he didn't, and then he could rescue his own damn butt.

"Of course, sweetheart, I did." He lifted a shoulder in the direction of the other two men. "Sorry, guys, looks like I just got a better offer than talking to you two clowns."

"Go for it, man," Ron said, then guzzled down the rest of his champagne. "Where's that waiter?"

Larry sighed. "I'm not driving you home again, pal."

Jill led Spenser toward the dance floor, feeling a tad bad about Efrem's stunned look. Out of the corner of her eye she saw that all three men continued to watch them as the guys talked among themselves, and she wondered if she actually had to go through with this dancing thing.

"My hero," Spenser whispered in her ear, and she heard the laughter in his voice, felt the shiver down her spine, the heat where she had no business feeling hot.

"Don't be so ungrateful." She glanced over her shoulder again. The three men still watched them, but she hesitated anyway.

"I'm very grateful. I'm bursting with gratitude, in fact," he said, grinning and tugging at her hand. "I know how much you're going to hate doing this."

She pulled free. "Don't get ahead of yourself. We don't have to actually get out there and make fools of ourselves."

"We won't do that," he assured her. And slipping an arm around her waist, he swept her onto the dance floor before she could put on the brakes.

The sensation, she guessed, was not unlike drowning. As soon as their feet hit the parquet and the other couples sashayed around them, swift panic robbed her of all common sense. Not even the sweet sound of Kenny G soothed her. She couldn't breathe, no matter how deeply she tried, and a light-headed feeling started to descend.

"You're doing great," he whispered. "Just follow me. We'll go slow."

"Great?" Her voice came out a squeak. "What do you mean *great?*" This time she spoke too loudly and several people glanced their way. "I can't do this," she hissed in a lower octave.

"You already are."

She inhaled a deep breath, tempted to look down at their feet, but Spenser was holding her too tightly and besides, she figured she might get dizzy if she got an actual look.

The music swirled around them and she felt herself starting to relax. His hand pressed to the small of her back proved a great comfort, as did the steady beat of his heart against her breast.

"This isn't so bad," she finally admitted. "At least if I flub up, I don't know anyone here."

"I'm surprised you care what anyone thinks. You seem so independent most of the time."

"Old habits," she murmured. "Comes with always being the new kid in school and being the center of attention. Not a pretty picture."

A slight frown puckered his eyebrows as he looked down at her, and she knew she'd surprised him by revealing that tidbit of information, but she had an ulterior motive. She wanted her own curiosity satisfied.

"Well, I think you're fairly safe here. Unless you either fly, build or sell some sort of aircraft, you shouldn't see anyone you know."

Right now, she barely cared. Spenser's arm around her was doing interesting things to her nervous system, not to mention the dizzying feeling she was experiencing by being pressed against him from thigh to shoulder. She had an overwhelming urge to kiss him, to make him kiss her. But she knew if she started something out here, in the middle of the floor, they were likely to end up being a spectacle for sure.

"Well, I *am* in the travel business," she said, trying to tamp down a telltale grin. She tilted her head farther back and his warm breath caressed her cheek, sending a wicked shiver of need down her spine. That did it. If they didn't get out of here quickly, she would make fools of them both. "I suppose it's possible I'd know someone. In which case I shouldn't stay out here *too* long."

Her voice sounded strange and breathy even to her, and when the corners of his eyes started to crinkle, she knew he was getting the idea.

"You're right," he said, staring down at her, his gaze roaming her face. "Old Efrem owns an airline, a couple of travel agencies, no telling who he's invited. Better we play it safe and disappear a while."

She nodded, her eyes hopelessly snagged by his. "What did you have in mind?"

"It's a surprise." He dropped his arm from around her waist, but kept a tight hold of her hand and started weaving them through the crowd and off the parquet floor.

Excitement simmered inside her, and she had trouble catching her next breath. Giddiness made her steps falter when his clip became too fast.

"Slow down," she pleaded, laughing. "I'm not going to change my mind."

"You're damn right."

His darkened eyes briefly met hers, and happiness bubbled within her like fine sparkling wine. She suddenly knew without a doubt that she'd follow this man anywhere. And if he asked her, she would gladly stay. Feeling this happy couldn't be wrong.

He flashed her a heart-stopping smile that cinched the deal.

It was at that second she saw him, over Spenser's shoulder, in front of the Christmas tree. The wavy black hair, the distinctive profile...there was no mistake.

When Maury turned in her direction, the laughter died in her throat.

12

"LET'S NOT GO that way." Jill stopped, and when it looked as though Spenser wouldn't, she jerked her hand out of his.

Slowly he turned to her, his gaze narrowed. "I thought you weren't going to change your mind."

"I haven't." She took a quick, deep breath, her gaze flickering in Maury's direction. He'd stopped to talk to a woman in a black fur-trimmed dress. He hadn't seen her. She knew that for certain. "I mean, I, uh, let's go look at the food."

Hurt clouded his eyes, and then he passed a hand over his face and the emotion was gone. "What just happened, Jill?"

"Can we discuss it later?"

"Do I have a choice?"

A waiter passed with a tray of champagne-filled glasses and Spenser lifted off a flute for himself. Jill grabbed it out of his hand and downed half the contents.

"Dancing sure makes you thirsty, huh?" she said, handing the glass back to him, her gaze straining over his shoulder to locate Maury. He'd moved closer to the tree.

When Spenser didn't take the flute, she met his eyes. "If you very calmly walk me to the back of the room, then around the other side of the tree and out the door, I promise I'll explain everything, answer any question you want, *do* anything you want."

Her gaze wandered over Spenser's shoulder again, seek-

ng her boss. His nose hovered over a tray of hors d'oeuvres
as he studied the morsels, trying to select one. She returned
her attention to Spenser. "Now would be a really good
time."

Irritation marked his expression. "What are you doing
to your hair?"

Her hand stilled. She'd been twisting her hair into a knot,
and she realized that she subconsciously knew what a bea-
con her mane of auburn curls would be for Maury. She had
to get out of here. Fast. With or without Spenser.

"You see someone you know, don't you?" Spenser
asked, turning to see what she'd been looking at.

Grabbing his arm, she hauled him around to face her
again. "Maury is here. I have to get the hell out of this
party."

"Maury? Your Maury?" He started to turn again.

She jerked his arm. "He's not my Maury. Don't turn
around." Placing her free hand on his chest, she scooted
down lower so that Spenser's body blocked hers from Maury's view. "In fact, don't move at all."

Quickly, she peeked over his shoulder before ducking
again. Maury had moved on to the selection of his next
morsel. He was one of the most self-absorbed people Jill
had ever encountered, and she knew it wouldn't matter to
him if a dozen people were waiting for a shot at the tray.
He'd take his time and select the very best. She figured she
had another forty-five seconds. Tops.

Spenser remained oddly silent and she frowned at him.
He looked slightly pained. "What's wrong?" she said.

"Uh, nothing that won't go away in a minute."

"I don't have time to play around, Spenser," she said,
groaning, and started to mumble a prayer she remembered
from grade school. She couldn't recall all the words, so she
made up a few. She cocked her head to the side, and saw

that Maury's back was partially to them as he shook hand
with someone.

She brought her head back in line with Spenser, her eye
even with his Adam's apple. "Okay," she whispered
"let's make a run for it."

"Wait."

"Wait?" Her gaze flew to his. He had that same awfu
look on his face. To her right, several people stared.

She blinked, and swept a glance to her left. More stares

Her hand flexed nervously on his chest. "Spenser
What—" She stopped. Her stomach somersaulted, and th
sick, bitter taste of realization coated her suddenly dr
mouth.

If she'd purposely tried, she couldn't have called mor
attention to them, plastered as she was to the front of him
Her thighs were molded to his, her breasts were presse
against his chest.

And Spenser was harder than a damn boulder.

Her breath left in a whoosh as she stumbled away fron
him.

Any other time, the hapless, stunned expression on hi
face would have sent her into hysterics. Right now, she
wanted to melt into the seams of the carpet.

"Spenser, I'm so…I'm, oh, God." She craned her necl
to see past him. Maury was headed their way. "I've got t
get out of here."

Spenser latched on to her arm. "Talk to him now, Jill
Tell him there isn't going to be a wedding."

"I can't do that."

"I don't mean in front of everyone. Pull him aside."

"Let go of my arm."

"It's the perfect time. He won't make a scene."

She shook free. Panic tightened her throat so that she

had to gasp for a breath. "You don't understand. It's not that simple."

"You have to grow up sometime, Jill," he said softly.

She gave him one final look, pleading for understanding, before she disappeared into the crowd.

AN HOUR LATER, Spenser began wondering if Jill had found another way home. He hadn't located her on the dance floor or in the small sitting room off the foyer. The car had been valet parked, and the attendants assured him she hadn't asked for the keys or the car.

He'd even staked out the ladies' room for nearly half an hour without any luck. And he'd already called home twice and had only gotten his own voice on the answering machine.

He scrubbed at his weary eyes. She'd been nothing but trouble from the first moment he met her. If he never saw her again, he'd probably be far better off. So why was he going out of his mind with worry? Why did he even give a damn where she was?

Who was he kidding?

Yeah, Jill had brought chaos to his orderly life, but she'd brought fun and enthusiasm, too. She'd also brought reminders. That being a good father meant more than adhering to a schedule, that being there for Mindy extended beyond physical presence.

And most important, Jill had shown him how to be his daughter's hero. He smiled, thinking about Mindy's face when all those kids had shown up for her party. And when he'd felt guilty about not knowing how isolated his child had become, he'd pushed it aside. Because Jill had taught him how to keep moving forward.

Now, he wanted to be Jill's hero.

A waiter stopped and Spenser waved off an offer of more champagne. He needed to keep a clear head.

"You must be getting old, Spenser," Efrem said, approaching him with a twinkle in his eye and a beer in his hand. "You used to be able to drink with the best of us, party till the end. You look like you've had it for tonight."

Spenser yanked the knot in his tie looser. "Have you seen Jill?"

"Ah, so it's the other explanation." The older man took a long pull of his beer, then grinned. "Love."

He grunted. "Love?"

Efrem's grin broadened. "I haven't seen her since you two hit the dance floor."

Nodding, Spenser swung a quick glance around the room, looking for a mane of auburn hair. When his gaze returned to his friend, he frowned at the way the man was eyeing him so closely.

Spenser paused for a moment, debating the wisdom of what he was about to ask. Depending on Efrem's relationship with the man, it could get sticky. "Look, Efrem, do you know some guy named Maury who owns a travel agency?"

The man's bushy white eyebrows drew together. "He owns more than a travel agency, but, yeah, I know him." His frown deepened. "You don't want to get mixed up with him, son."

An eerie feeling slithered across the back of Spenser's neck. He'd known Efrem a long time. The jovial old guy rarely looked this serious. "It's nothing like that. I don't even know the man." He loosened his tie another fraction. "Why? Why not get mixed up with him?"

Efrem ditched his empty beer bottle on a nearby table, then looked Spenser directly in the eyes. In a lowered voice, he said, "He's offering big money for your design, isn't he?"

"I swear to you, I never heard of the man until a week ago, and even then, it had nothing to do with my work."

The older man regarded him for a long silent moment, as if measuring him. "He's bad news. Word is, he's mob-related."

Spenser massaged the back of his neck and squinted at the ceiling, trying to remember. Something teased his memory.

"Nothing's been proven, of course," Efrem continued, shrugging. "You might remember that little scandal a few years back where Maury sued a reporter for slander when she wrote an article implying his connection. After that, the issue died. But there's quite a few of us who've stayed cautious."

"So why invite him to your party?"

"I do a little business with him when I have to. He's in the import-export business as well as small-craft charters. Besides, he's not someone you want to piss off, if you know what I mean."

Spenser did know. But he didn't like it. He wondered how much Jill was privy to. The idea that she knew anything at all about her employer's possible shady dealings made him sick.

No, she couldn't be involved. Not Jill. She was trying to get away from the creep, wasn't she? Besides, she might be blunt or impulsive or...

Realization jabbed him and he tugged at his necktie. It was beginning to feel more like a noose. Impulsiveness could get someone in an awful lot of trouble.

"Point him out," he said, his gaze continually scanning the room.

"Why the interest?"

Spenser thought about his answer for a moment, but he saw no reason not to trust his friend with a few minor details. "Between you and me, Jill used to work for the guy and she's not anxious to come face-to-face with him."

"Ah." Stroking his goatee, Efrem nodded and started skimming faces. "Smart lady."

"She may have already made it out of here, but if you see her, let me know. Quietly, of course."

"That's him."

Spenser's gaze flew to Efrem's face. Inconspicuously, the older man nudged his bearded chin to the right, his eyes trained on a trio of men at the head of the buffet table.

Near the reindeer ice sculpture, one man in particular stood out. He wore a tuxedo, whereas few others did, and at his throat was a red silk bow tie that matched his cummerbund.

"Let me guess," Spenser said dryly, sizing up the guy.

Efrem smiled. "I'd stay away from him if I were you," he said, and waved to a platinum-blond woman in a skintight black dress. "Now, if you'll excuse me..."

Spenser was only scarcely aware of his host's departure. He was too enthralled with watching the sleazeball who'd had the gall to think someone like Jill would marry him for any reason.

On sight he didn't like the guy. Not just because of his association with Jill, although the idea did stick in Spenser's craw, but because he looked arrogant. It was hard picturing Jill even working for this guy, especially with her smart mouth. The thought made Spenser smile in spite of himself.

A group of people moved between him and the sleazeball and Spenser automatically stepped around them to get closer to the three men. He didn't want to talk with them, or even eavesdrop, but he figured if he couldn't find Jill, he'd at least be assured that they hadn't found her, either.

He sidestepped a couple carrying plates of food and declined a drink offer from a passing waiter. Again the trio were in his immediate path when the man dressed as Santa got in the way.

Spenser groaned in frustration, and Santa tried to hand him a cigar. "No, thanks," Spenser said as civilly as his impatience would allow, and moved to the side, keeping sight of Maury.

"May I have one of those?" the man in back of Spenser asked.

Sighing, Santa shoved one at him.

"And a rose for my date?" the man added.

Santa growled, covered it up with a ho-ho-ho and tossed three roses toward the woman.

Spenser stopped and abruptly turned. He'd recognize that growl anywhere.

"You don't have to be rude," the woman said, her sharply arched eyebrows scrunching up as she peered closely at Santa.

"Right. Have a cigar." Santa handed the woman the box, then used his free hand to hike up his sagging trousers. From behind a pair of wire-rimmed spectacles, striking violet eyes met Spenser's.

"Jill." He kept his voice low so that only she could hear, his gaze flicking toward Maury.

The couple moved on while exchanging puzzled looks.

"It ain't the Easter Bunny." She passed out two more roses.

"Keep heading in this direction." Stepping up beside her, he narrowly stopped himself from cupping her elbow. "Maury is behind you by the buffet."

She slid him a swift sideways look and kept moving

through the crowd. "I know where he is. How do you know *who* he is? You didn't—" She cut herself off. "Never mind. Of course you didn't."

"I didn't," he said, not quite sure what she was babbling about. "I assume you still want to get the hell out of here."

"What, no lecture on running away?"

"Not in this case."

She gave him an odd look, then passed out another rose.

"Good. Keep passing those out so you don't look suspicious." *Oh no.* Spenser had a horrible thought. He leaned subtly toward her. "You didn't mug anybody for the suit, did you?"

"No, but you owe the guy a hundred bucks."

He chuckled. "No problem."

"What's His Highness doing now?"

He hesitated, then catching her meaning, he glanced over his shoulder at Maury. "Eating."

"Perfect." As soon as they stepped onto the marble foyer, she unloaded the remaining roses on a balding man with a crooked mustache and a bewildered look on his face. "Let's head for the door."

"Where's your dress?"

"The real Santa's holding it hostage for the suit and his money."

"Smart guy."

"Ready?"

"I've already got the valet ticket in my hand."

"Spenser?"

They stopped, waiting for the automatic glass doors to yawn open, and he turned to look at her. A blast of cold air whizzed in, and she shivered.

"Yes?" He slipped an arm around her shoulders. He didn't care what anyone thought.

"I owe you," she said softly, her lower lip quivering. "Big time."

He smiled. "Yes, you do. And tonight, I intend to collect."

ILL LET the Santa suit bottoms fall to her ankles, then stepped out of them. She still wore the thigh-high black hose, but that was the last evidence of her Cinderella evening. She couldn't even collect her dress until tomorrow.

She picked the suit up off the floor and stared moodily at the heap of gray sweatpants she'd left sitting on the pink floral-chintz chair. She was tired of wearing those old shapeless things. Spenser deserved to see her in something nicer.

Especially since she had to leave tomorrow.

The thought pierced her heart like the fine tip of a steel dart. She shoved the pain aside. It wasn't as if she had a choice. No telling who could have seen her tonight. For all she knew, Maury may have already gotten the word that she was still in town.

Tomorrow night, while the Montagues celebrated Christmas Eve, she'd get her things from the mall and clean out her apartment. By Christmas Day, she figured she'd hit Kansas.

A soft knock at the door roused her. She knew it was Spenser. Mindy was spending the night at her grandmother's. They were alone in the house. He had seen to that. The thought sent a shiver of sweet anticipation down to her belly.

"I'll be right out," she called, reaching for a sweatshirt. "Meet me in the living room."

She frowned at the closed door as she pulled the shirt over her head. They never used the living room.

Curiosity made her hurry and she was bounding dow
the stairs a minute later.

She heard the fire crackle in the hearth a moment befor
she rounded the corner. The flickering light from the flame
was the only illumination in the room as she entered. Sper
ser stoked the logs with a brass poker and a shower c
miniature fireworks erupted into the semidarkness, momer
tarily lighting his face. He appeared solemn, as though h
had a lot on his mind.

"You really did mean the living room, huh?" she askec
feeling a sudden and unaccountable nervousness.

Chuckling, he set the poker aside. "Yeah, but don't te
Mindy. I don't think she knows about it."

"She really doesn't have to stay at your mom's over
night."

"Yes, she does."

"Oh." She rubbed her hands together and looked idl
around. "Well..."

He put out a hand. "Come here."

Jill swallowed. She wasn't usually shy about this sort c
thing, but she was suddenly having trouble getting her leg
to work properly. Slowly, she moved toward him. As soo
as she got near the fireplace, she saw the large dark shadov
in the corner.

Startled, she straightened, then realized what it was.

A bare pine stood about six feet, its graceful limbs em
bracing the air to form a perfect triangle.

"There's a big tree over there," she said, and h
laughed.

"Yeah, I know. It's customary at this time of year t
have them."

"But...when did...I don't—" She squinted at him. "It'
not decorated."

Reaching behind a chair, he dragged out a cardboard bo

and smiled. "I'm sure you can take care of that in no time."

"Spenser," she drawled in admonishment, looking from the box to him to the pine. Beyond that, words failed her, and she nibbled at her lower lip. Finally, she said, "We should wait for Mindy."

"Nope. This is your tree, Jill."

"My tree," she murmured, her heart picking up speed. This was silly. She was a grown woman. She should not be this thrilled about a damn pine.

Dropping to her knees, she threw open the box's cardboard flaps. A wild assortment of funky ornaments had been carefully laid out between layers of tissue paper.

She picked up the red Mardi Gras mask in one hand, the miniature stuffed bear in the other, and stared at them for a moment before transferring her gaze to Spenser's pleased face. "Where did you get these?"

"I bought them."

"You?"

"I'll try not to take your skepticism as an insult."

She laughed and turned back to sift through the box. Mickey Mouse swung from a Christmas wreath, Daffy Duck was peeking into a semiwrapped present and a witch rode a broom. She peered more closely at the witch. The small figure had red hair suspiciously similar to hers, and Jill slid Spenser a dubious glare. He smiled, the flickering fire giving him a devilish look.

She laughed as she pushed herself up. She couldn't help it. Delirious happiness made her giddy. She had no doubt she still had explaining to do about Maury and the entire evening, but not only had Spenser given her a temporary reprieve, he'd given her a Christmas tree. No one had ever done anything like that for her before.

He took her hands and finished helping her to her feet,

urging her close enough for him to slide his arms around her. She looped hers around his neck and knew she could never tire of gazing at this man.

"I don't know what to say," she whispered.

"This has to be a first."

She lightly punched his shoulder, and laughing, he snagged her arm and returned it to its place around his neck.

"To be honest, I didn't have talking in mind," he said, and then he kissed her.

13

SPENSER HAD QUESTIONS, many questions. They had a lot to discuss. But that could all wait. Right now, he was just too damn glad she was here safe with him.

He pressed his hand lightly at the curve of her back and her entire body responded, pressing urgently against him, making him struggle for control.

Her lips parted slightly beneath his and when he teased her lower one with his tongue, her soft moan was nearly his undoing.

He took one final small nip, then pulled back.

Her eyes seemed unfocused as she blinked at him.

"Let's go upstairs," he said, bringing one hand up to cup her face. Her skin was like fine silk and he dragged the pad of his thumb across her cheek to absorb the softness.

Slowly, she shook her head, her eyes beginning to brighten.

His gut clenched. Had he read her so wrong?

"I don't want to leave my tree," she said, smiling, and he relaxed. "The carpet looks rather durable, don't you think?"

"Very," he agreed, brushing back an errant curl.

Her smile wavered for a moment and she brought one arm down from around his neck to place her palm against his chest. "And I want to explain something first. About Maury."

Spenser smirked to himself. This morning, or even an hour ago, he would have given anything for Jill to have introduced the topic of her own volition. But at this particular moment, he was less than thrilled with the prospect of discussing that sleaze.

"Sure," he said, taking a deep breath, then leading her toward the couch.

She settled down next to him, but her posture was as stiff as a drafting board. He reached around her and kneaded her shoulders.

She closed her eyes. "I could get used to this."

"That's the idea."

Her lids promptly lifted. "There's more you need to know about Maury."

He kept kneading. "I think maybe I already do."

She frowned and shifted so that he couldn't easily reach her and he let his hand fall away. "Such as?"

"You go first."

She scooted back and drew her legs up, hugging them to herself. "I told you the truth about him wanting to marry me for tax reasons and how we'd already gone through this last year and the year before, but..." She stopped, her frown deepening. "What do you know about him?"

"But?" he prompted.

"I'm not trying to stall," she said, lifting her chin. "It's just that this year he seems so much more determined."

He could tell she was holding something back, so he didn't respond, hoping she would continue.

"What is it you know about Maury?" she asked again.

He smiled to himself. She wasn't going to give up. "About his mob connections."

"His what?" Her eyes widened like a frightened doe's. "That's just rumor. I don't believe it."

"You don't think there's any truth to it at all?"

She vigorously shook her head, then stared hard at the far wall. An erratic assortment of emotions paraded across her face. Then her entire body seemed to sag and fear flashed in her eyes before she shuttered it. "The whole idea is ridiculous," she added in a tone that lacked conviction.

"Talk to me, Jill."

"I've known him for almost three years. He has a desk near mine. You think I wouldn't know if he was mixed up in something shady?" Her eyebrows furrowed and she chewed her lower lip. "Where did you get this information?"

"Don't get excited. I know it's only rumor. I'm just glad you don't have anything more to do with him. But you had something else you were going to tell me," he reminded her.

"What?" She blinked at him, and he got the distinct impression she wasn't hearing a thing he said. "No. I, uh, that was all...just that he was so adamant about getting married this time." She looked away. "That's why he didn't want me to go."

"Where did he think you were going? To visit family?"

"No, he knows I don't have any."

"I'm sorry." There was so much he didn't know about her.

"That came out wrong." She waved an agitated hand. "I have a father and a brother, but they both live abroad. They're in the army. I haven't seen them in years."

"And your mother?"

"She died."

He took her hand. It was as cold as an icicle. "When?"

"I'm not sure." She cocked her head to the side and stared into the semidarkness. "Probably when I was about five or six." When she looked at him again, she must have seen the surprise in his face, because she hastily added, "I don't mean to sound flip. I didn't know she was dead until a long time later. My father had only said she went away."

Granted, it happened a long time ago, but her calm, almost clinical acceptance unnerved him. "Did he lie to you on purpose?"

Her lips turned down at the corners. "My dad's a drunk. His way of grieving was to crawl into a bottle. He didn't mean to deliberately hurt us."

"But he did."

She shrugged. "I wish I hadn't grown up thinking she'd deserted us. Every time we moved, I was terribly worried she wouldn't be able to find us. But that's all history now."

She lied. The pain wasn't as neatly tucked away in the past as she wanted to believe. Spenser could see it in the tentative way she'd moved her shoulders, the way sadness shadowed her eyes. He thought about his own daughter, and how painful her mother's leaving was for her. He hurt for both her and Jill.

"Besides, there was an upshot to all that moving around," Jill said, the beginnings of a smile tugging at her lips. "I got to see the world and it kept my mind off things. Sometimes I even liked it, especially when I got older."

"Of course you did. It allowed you to run away from responsibility instead of facing it."

She blinked, the smile fading from her face. Unfolding her legs, she started to leave the couch, but he laid a hand on her arm and stopped her. He saw no merit in voicing the fact that she was proving his point by trying to get away. He was irritated with himself for having unwisely made the remark in the first place.

"I'm sorry. That was uncalled for," he said. "Don't go. You have your tree to decorate."

"You don't play fair, do you?" She sank back down, her expression a cross between amusement and frustration.

"If it's too important to win, you're right, I don't." He adn't released her yet, and he tugged her toward him. When she finally budged, he was relieved to find her moving closer. She sagged against him as though suddenly one-tired.

"What do you hope to win?" she asked cautiously.

"You," he said, cupping her face with one hand and ightly brushing his lips across hers.

Jill closed her eyes. It would be so easy to push away ll the unpleasantness concerning Maury, she thought as penser trailed a string of tiny kisses along her jaw. She elt safe here, being with him, talking to him, kissing him.

She couldn't ever remember feeling this way before. But he wasn't a fool, and she knew that the only thing more angerous to her than Maury was this false safety she felt.

She had to leave, now more than ever. Even Spenser had eard the rumors, which really made her nervous. She idn't want to believe them herself, but too much was starting to add up.

She wanted to explain her uneasiness to Spenser, but hat did she honestly have to tell him? That Maury had ired goons? That she suspected there was something trange about that last deposit she'd made? That maybe it ad something to do with the payroll check she'd cashed? he herself had more questions than answers. And he had lindy to think about. He couldn't afford to get involved n Jill's problems. And knowing him, he'd probably want o jump in and fix things for her. Disappearing was the best hing she could do for both of them.

But not until tomorrow.

"What are you thinking?" he whispered as he leaned ack and watched her stare at the fireplace, entranced by ne flames licking the charred wood.

Transfixed, she had trouble dragging her gaze away, but

she finally did, smiling at him. "That we've just wasted an awful lot of time talking."

Relief, desire, both converged on his face at once. "You're right," he said, and kissed her again.

This time there was nothing gentle or teasing or tame about their union. She sensed a long-suppressed hunger that created urgency in the way he prodded her lips apart, the way he urged her back against the couch. His tongue dived and swept and made her so dizzy she gratefully reclined against the cushions.

This new position made access to his shirt buttons easy, and she plucked them free, one by one, until his chest was bare and she feverishly raked her fingers through the soft black hair carpeting well-toned muscles.

His nipples were as aroused as her own and they beaded against her palm, making her crazy with need. She wanted to feel his naked body pressed to hers. She wanted nothing standing between them. She wanted to carry this feeling of being cared for locked away in her heart for the rest of her life.

Because after tomorrow, the memory would be all she'd have.

"Jill," he murmured, his breath ragged and warm against her skin, and she suddenly realized that he'd yanked up her sweatshirt and was trying to remove it.

She immediately lifted her arms, and after pulling off the shirt, he cast it aside, across the room, near the foot of the tree.

She giggled.

"What's so funny?" His voice was hoarse, raspy.

"You're being a slob. I never thought I'd see—"

He didn't let her finish. Kissing her hard, he reached down and easily tugged the too-big sweatpants down her hips, then flung them past the shirt. He pulled back and smiled.

"You're not laughing anymore," he whispered, then started nuzzling her neck while he reached for her bra hook.

"Shut up, Noah." She pushed his shirt off his shoulders. Before it slid from his back, she started on his belt buckle. His deep, vibrating laughter stroked her skin.

He wouldn't stop kissing or nuzzling and she couldn't see what she was doing. But she managed to unbuckle, unsnap and unzip in short order.

Having already unfastened her bra, he didn't hesitate to help her rid himself of his jeans and in seconds they were both gloriously naked, stretched out on the couch, her breasts pressed to his chest as she lay atop him.

His hands glided slowly down her back to cup her buttocks and her skin tingled in their wake. He was hard beneath her, his desire nudging her belly, and she wiggled a little, teasing him, taunting him, driving herself crazy.

"Hey, you." His laugh was a short, hoarse bark that danced across her collarbone and licked at her sensitive nerve endings.

"Hey, what?"

"Talk about not playing fair."

She grinned. "But am I winning?"

He reached between them and probed between her thighs. "You tell me," he whispered.

She shifted against his fingers and lost her balance. He tried to steady her with the arm he still had wrapped around her, but she rolled off him onto the carpet, sputtering, laughing, until he followed her down.

"I told you we should have gone upstairs," he said, kicking the coffee table farther away while trying to hold her with one arm. They had cleared the glass and brass by mere inches.

"Where's your sense of adventure?"

"Trekking south of the equator at the moment."

She started to laugh, but ended up sucking in her breath as his mouth closed around a nipple. The tip of his tongue exacted a revenge she found both unbearable and exquisite and she moaned softly until she felt him smile against her

"You're so incredibly soft," he whispered.

"Thank goodness *you* aren't."

He laughed. "Jill, don't ever change. I like you blunt and impulsive and just a little mouthy."

"Tell me that in the morning," she said, teasing him but not because she thought he was like so many other guys who would say anything in the heat of the moment.

He tongued the tip of her other breast. "I'll say it tomorrow morning." He nipped gently. "The next morning." Her nipple disappeared into his mouth. "And the morning after that."

Her breath caught in her throat. She wouldn't think about tomorrow. She wouldn't ruin tonight that way.

"Spenser?"

"Hmm..."

"Let's go upstairs."

He suckled deeply before looking at her, a dark lock of hair falling across his eyebrow, a shadow of uncertainty in his eyes. A small hesitant frown tugged at his expression. "Is something wrong?"

Slowly she shook her head. "I figure we're in for a long night."

A wicked grin stretched across his face as he got to his feet and pulled her up with him. "I believe the term is long, *hard* night."

WHEN THE FAINT salmon-colored rays of dawn barged their way between the slanted miniblinds, Jill was tempted to pull Spenser's black satin sheets over her head and pretend today wasn't Christmas Eve.

Instead, she snuggled closer to his warm naked body and told herself how grateful she should be for having had last night with him at all. He breathed deeply in his sleep and she gently placed her hand on top of his chest as it rose and fell. Somehow she felt calmed by his heart beating strongly against her palm.

He stirred. "How long have you been awake?" he asked, his voice thick with sleep.

"I woke you," she whispered, glancing up at him. She hadn't meant to do that. She'd just wanted to touch him.

His eyes were hooded, his chin stubbly. A lazy smile inched across his face. "Don't sound so disappointed. A lot of interesting things can happen when I'm up."

She grinned at his suggestive tone. "You are a very bad boy."

He nudged her shoulder a little until she shifted and he was able to work his arm beneath her. The sheets were smooth and slick, and he easily slid her flush against him, his arm still hooked around her waist.

"I have a feeling you like bad boys," he said after kissing the top of her head.

"Now, why would you think that?" she asked, tracing a pattern around his peaking nipple.

"Just a hunch."

She stilled her fingers and looked at him, suddenly a little disturbed. "I swear to you that there was never anything between Maury and me."

Fisting a hand around hers, he brought her fingers to his lips and swiftly kissed the tips. "Honey, I wasn't implying that at all. Maury was the furthest thing from my mind."

She sighed. "I'm sorry. I don't know why I'm so touchy."

When she started to leave the bed, he tightened his hold. "Come on. Let's not ruin our morning with talk of Maury. He's history, right?"

"Uh-huh," she mumbled, and tried to relax against him. Spenser was right. If she started thinking about Maury, and tonight, and how she was never going to see Spenser or Mindy again, she would lose it. Her throat tightened at the thought.

"You're cold," he said, cuddling her impossibly closer. "You're shivering."

She forced a laugh. "Normal people have flannel sheets on their bed this time of year."

"You don't like these?"

She elbowed him until he jumped and started laughing. He knew she did. They had spent hours tangling in the luxurious satin. They'd even shared a private joke or two about the slippery appeal of the fabric.

"Okay, I admit it," she said in a grudging tone. "You're not quite the stuffed shirt I initially thought you were."

"You thought I was what?" he asked, his free hand snaking below the covers.

"Hey. Knock it off." She tried to dodge his intimate assault on her naked breasts. She didn't try too hard, though, and sighed when he found his target. "How can I defend myself if you're doing that?"

"Want me to stop?"

Her eyes briefly fluttered closed. "I'll break your arm."

He laughed, and she ducked in to kiss him on the chin. She wanted to keep watching him the rest of the morning. He looked younger somehow…relaxed was probably more accurate. He wasn't Mindy's father or the guy who everyone seemed to think should still be flying planes. He was her lover; she wanted to wrap that knowledge around her like a warm fuzzy blanket and never let it go.

"Spenser?" She flattened her palm on his chest, rested her chin on top of it and gazed at him. "Why don't you still fly?"

His eyebrows puckered and it was clear this wasn't a subject he liked to discuss. "I can't be away from Mindy."

"Other single fathers work outside the home."

"Flying isn't a nine-to-five job. I could be gone for days, almost a week at a time." He shook his head, and although he did it with finality, a wistful longing briefly crossed his face. "Mindy needs the reassurance that I'll be here at the end of each day."

Jill studied the way his mouth set. There'd be no discussing the matter. His mind was made up. Not that she had any right to try and change it. Still, she was a little curious yet, and sad that he'd given up so much. "Do you think putting your life on hold is good for Min? I mean, as far as being an example."

"I was an engineer before I started flying. This new engine design I've been working on could save lives." He pushed a hand through his hair, suddenly looking weary. "I'm not exactly wasting my life here."

"I didn't mean to imply that." She rolled off him and settled back against the oak headboard, pulling the covers up around her breasts. "I just think it's a shame you aren't doing what you love."

"Yeah, sometimes responsibility is hell, isn't it?"

Their eyes met, his dark and probing, and unease pricked Jill's conscience. It would be foolish to take what he'd just said—or didn't say—personally. They were talking about him, not her. Leaving didn't mean she was irresponsible. She was, after all, concerned about his and Mindy's welfare, too.

"Hey, you look so serious all of a sudden." He reached out and cupped the side of her face. "That's not allowed on Christmas Eve. What would Santa say if he knew one of his helpers was looking so blue?''

She smiled and pressed her face into his palm. He was right. There was no sense in ruining their last few hours together.

Their last few hours. The thought made her breath catch, and she used every once of willpower she possessed to keep her smile intact.

He didn't seem to notice as he shifted closer to her.

"You know, Mindy isn't coming home until this afternoon," he said, his lips grazing her jaw, the stubble on his chin tickling the side of her neck. "And if you're really good, I have a feeling Santa just may come early."

Sighing, she closed her eyes. And for the first time since she was six years old, she truly wanted to believe.

MINDY LOOKED so adorable in her red velvet Christmas dress with the ivory-lace bib that Jill felt her eyes begin to mist. Behind the little girl, the family-room Christmas tree shone brightly with hundreds of colorful lights.

Sitting contentedly on the leather wingchair with her legs drawn up beneath her, Jill watched the child pirouette in front of her father, then was surprised when Mindy ran over to give her a hug and a kiss.

"What was that for?" she asked, blinking rapidly to eliminate any signs of her wistfulness.

"I want you to come with us to Grandma's tonight," Mindy said, sticking out her chin. "You gotta come. We get to open at least one present, maybe two, and drink eggnog and eat Christmas cake with strawberry icing. It won't be the same without you."

"Eggnog and cake? Oh, good, just what you need, more sugar."

"Careful," Spenser said, a mock frown on his face. "You're sounding like the G-word again."

"Will you come?" Mindy's pleading turned to whining.

Jill glanced at Spenser for help. He offered none. She knew he didn't understand why she'd refused to go with them. "I told you, I have too much to do. Santa needs me at the North Pole in an hour."

"Maybe you can call and tell him you'll be late?"

"But if I do that, then you might not get your presents

tonight," Jill said, and had to hide a grin when she saw alarm widen Mindy's eyes.

Then the child's forehead slowly creased, and she said "That's okay. If you go with us, I'll get part of my wish."

Jill's heart swelled to her throat and her gaze flew to meet Spenser's. A fresh surge of emotion started to well up behind her eyes.

He smiled, and said, "Mine, too."

She set her feet on the floor and pushed off the chair so abruptly that she startled Mindy. "That's fine for you two to say. I'm the one who'd be out of a job."

"Mindy, why don't you go and look for your good gloves?" Spenser said. "I think they're on the shelf in your closet."

"But, Daddy, I want Jill to come with us."

"Young lady, tonight of all nights is not a good time for you to be arguing, is it?" He lifted a stern eyebrow, and his daughter wisely headed for her room.

As soon as she was out of earshot, he turned to Jill and asked, "Aren't you taking the Santa's-helper thing a little too far? We won't be at my mother's all that long, if that's what's worrying you. She knows Mindy has to get to bed early."

She shrugged and picked at the hem of her sweatshirt. "This is a family thing. I wouldn't feel right."

Stepping close, he circled his arms around her, held her against his chest and kissed the top of her head, before resting his chin there. "You are family. Don't you know that?"

"Don't."

His hold loosened, and Jill immediately regretted her tone. She hadn't meant to sound so sharp. But he was making this so hard for her. She had to leave. She had no choice. If he knew the whole story, he would understand that. But he didn't know, and she couldn't tell him.

"What's wrong, Jill?" he asked, pulling back to look at her, one hand still gripping her upper arm. "Are you sorry about last night, this morning?"

Miserable, she stared back and tried to come up with the right words to say. But seeing the genuine concern in his face, her defenses started to crumble. He cared about her. For once in her life, someone gave a damn about Jill Morgan.

Her knees got a little weak at the idea, and strange thoughts started tumbling through her head.

Why couldn't she tell him more about Maury? Would he hate her because she'd possibly put him and Mindy in danger? She wouldn't blame him. But she owed him more than a sudden disappearance. Didn't she? Oh, hell. Maybe he was right. Maybe she really was growing up.

She moistened her lips and smiled. "I will never be sorry about last night. Whatever happens, please don't ever think that last night was a mistake. Making love with you was...it was—"

His hand tightened around her arm, his fingers digging into her. "What do you mean...whatever happens?"

She shifted her arm, and obviously realizing how firm his grip was, he let her go. She took a deep breath. It was now or never. "There's something else you should know about Maury."

"I'm listening," he said, his sudden stern expression taking a large bite out of her confidence.

"Well, I don't have any proof, but I think he wants more from me than to say 'I do.'" Rubbing her arm, she paced a few steps away from him. "That day I met you, two guys were following me and I lost them at the mall. Other than just wanting to get out of town, I didn't think too much of it at the time. Maury hates to lose and I figured that since this was our third year of playing hide-and-seek, he was just getting irritated.''

For a moment he thought about what she'd said, then asked, ''What's changed your mind?''

''What you said about his mob connections. It gives me the creeps.''

He smiled, looking somewhat relieved. ''*Possible* connections. You said yourself you don't believe it. I don't think you need to panic yet.''

''But he was really ticked about the money.''

''Money?''

''I made a deposit, just like I always do.'' She shrugged. ''But it was a really big deposit, and Maury was furious that I'd made it earlier than usual. I have a feeling that money was never supposed to get to the bank.''

''And?'' He ducked his head to look her squarely in the eyes.

Damn, he was already getting to know her too well. ''That's it. I took off,'' she said, and turned away. She didn't know why she didn't tell him about cashing her check. But how important could that be? She'd exchanged her payroll check for cash twice before. Maury had never had a problem with that practice.

Sliding him a private look, she saw that his jaw was set and she knew what he was thinking. That she was an irresponsible wimp for running the way she had. But he didn't understand. She hadn't had much time to think of alternatives.

''Do you think you're in danger?''

''No. Not really. But obviously I'm in no hurry to see Maury again.''

''But of course you have to. Not right away. Maybe the day after Christmas.''

She gaped at him. "Why would I want to do that?"

"Because you can't keep looking over your shoulder." His gaze flickered over her. "Or wearing my sweatpants for the rest of your life because you're too afraid to go to your apartment."

She frowned. "What if I *do* have something to worry about?"

"We talk to the police. Maury won't bother you once he knows they're involved." He massaged his temple. "Look, we need to think this through, then decide our best course of action. Once I get home tonight and put Mindy to bed, we'll talk some more."

She nodded, not because she agreed, but because doing so avoided conflict.

He smiled. "After that, we'll decorate your tree."

Sadness sliced through her. Sudden memories of why they hadn't gotten around to the tree last night clawed at her heart and threatened to undermine her resolve.

But he was right. She didn't want to have to look over her shoulder. Or worry about putting him or Mindy in jeopardy. And skipping town would take care of both problems, she thought dejectedly as she watched him leave the family room.

After all, for twenty-eight years, leaving had solved most of her problems. Besides, Jill realized with sudden staggering clarity, she didn't know how to do anything else.

THE MALL was jumping with last-minute shoppers as Jill pushed through the revolving doors and headed down the main concourse toward the lockers. It hadn't occurred to her until a minute ago that if her things were no longer there, she didn't know what she was going to do about getting to her apartment. She'd just used the last twenty dollars Spenser had given her a few days ago to pay the taxi driver, and it was entirely possible that her belongings had been confiscated because of the length of time she'd left them.

She wasn't going to worry about something that may not be a problem yet, she told herself, and glanced over her shoulder. No sign of Maury or his goons. Although she didn't really expect to see them. She felt fairly confident that he'd given up by now. At least for Christmas Eve, anyway.

She tugged Spenser's navy-blue ski hat over her ears, making sure it covered most of her hair. All those red curls were like a calling card she didn't want or need right now. In a few days, once she was a few states away, she'd send the cap back to Spenser, along with his clothes.

Thoughts of him brought an unwelcome rush of emotion and she stopped to stare at a display window while she inconspicuously dabbed at her eyes. She'd left people behind before, and it had been difficult at times. But never had the pain been so acute as it was right now.

She stomped her foot in irritation. A man holding hands with two little girls had stopped to look at the display, but instead gave Jill an odd look and quickly moved on.

She watched them go, feeling even more miserable. He reminded her of Spenser. Not in looks, but in his protectiveness to his children.

Swallowing hard, she glanced around. Although it was mostly adults rushing in and out of stores, a few children tagged along, chattering happily, their eyes round and wide, looking at the decorated trees, carrying shopping bags that were way too big for them. And Jill's heartstrings tangled into several knots.

She'd never wanted a family before last week. She did now. She wanted Mindy. She wanted Spenser.

Stomping her foot one final time for good measure, she

swiped at the moisture around her eyes, then pushed off in the direction of the lockers.

Damn that Spenser. He made it sound so simple. As though staying and facing Maury would straighten everything out. It was fine for him to be so cavalier about all this. Spenser knew exactly what he wanted. Mindy needed a father at home, so he quit flying.

But that's *not* what he wanted, a small, nagging voice reminded her. He'd merely owned up to his responsibility. Pushing blindly through the crowd, Jill shoved the thought aside.

If it were so damn easy, her father would have stuck around. He wouldn't have checked out on her by crawling into a bottle. Nothing was easy. And she was doing the best she could.

So why did her best suddenly not feel good enough?

She'd been so lost in thought that she nearly passed the hallway that led to the lockers. After a quick, satisfied peek over her shoulder, she ducked into the short corridor and swiftly located her unit. Inserting the key into the lock, she held her breath, briefly closed her eyes and turned. The door sprung open, and crammed into the narrow space was her duffel bag, purse and a heap of clothes, just as she had left them.

Sending up a quick prayer of thanks, she gathered her things and rushed out into the wave of frenzied shoppers.

It was a little difficult at first, maneuvering the bag through the throng, but she made it to the revolving doors within a couple of minutes and immediately spotted the yellow taxi behind a dark sedan. She'd asked the driver to wait, promising him an extra twenty on top of the normal fare to her apartment if he did.

As soon as she threw her things onto the back seat and climbed in beside them, she took a deep, steadying breath and gave him the address to her apartment. Although it wasn't a long ride there, sitting in the growing darkness, alone with her thoughts, her mind kept playing tricks on her.

Distant memories of her father's drunken attempts to explain why they had to suddenly move again kept overlapping with thoughts of Spenser and Mindy. The idea was laughable, even to allow her father and Spenser to be on the same wavelength. The two men were nothing alike. Spenser embraced responsibility. Her father ran from it.

Just like me.

Jill closed her eyes and, sighing, she sunk lower in the seat. Life had been much easier before meeting Spenser. At least her conscience had never pricked like a bristly cactus.

We'll decide our best course of action, he'd said. He wasn't throwing her to the wolves. He was willing to help her find a solution, and still she was running. Did she want to follow her father's lead for the rest of her life?

The thought chafed. Besides, if she ran, this time she'd leave casualties. Just as her father had. Mindy would miss her. She wouldn't understand Jill's actions. She'd only know that someone had left her again.

And Spenser. He'd never forgive Jill.

She gasped for air. She didn't know if she could forgive herself.

"Okay, here you go, lady."

She jerked at the sound of the cabdriver's voice. He flipped on the interior light and with a gnarled brown finger, he tapped the meter. "You owe me twelve bucks, plus the extra twenty. And don't forget the usual fifteen percent tip."

Her hand groped for the door handle as her gaze wandered toward the dimly lit tan apartment building she'd called home for three years.

"Lady, are you getting out, or what?"

Slowly she shook her head. "I guess it's or what," she said, sliding her hand off the metal handle and sinking back against the cracked leather seat.

God, she hated this. Spenser was right. She was growing up.

ONLY ONE LAMP shone from inside the house. The outside Christmas lights woven throughout the shrubs were on a timer and automatically switched off at midnight, so that didn't give Jill any clue as to whether Spenser and Mindy had returned yet.

She hoped they were still at his mother's. If they were home, she thought, cringing, then Spenser had already read her note. He'd know she had planned on leaving for good.

"Come on, lady. It's Christmas Eve. I wanna go home. You gonna wait until New Year's to pay me?" The taxi driver let out a disgusted sigh.

"Keep your pants on," she said, and started digging through her purse. Even though she knew she was doing the right thing, she wasn't entirely happy about the prospect of facing Maury, and this guy and his speedy driving had gotten on her nerves.

Finally locating her wallet, she withdrew a wad of crisp new bills. Normally, she didn't carry so much money, but he'd cashed her payroll check for her trip out of town.

She peeled off several twenties, but the bills were so new she had trouble separating them and, instead of fussing with them, she gave the driver an inflated tip. "Merry Christmas," she said, handing him the fare, and suddenly feeling a little giddy. Tomorrow, Christmas, she'd be waking up with Spenser...if he didn't kick her out first.

"Hey, lady, thanks." He grinned, one gold tooth gleaming in the moonlight. "Anything else in the back seat?" he asked.

"Nope." She picked up the duffel bag she'd set on the sidewalk. "I've got everything."

He put his car into gear and she watched him speed down the road before she turned back to study the semidark house. Next door, a curtain fluttered and she smiled, knowing that Spenser's neighbor and self-appointed watchdog, Mrs. Peyton, was keeping tabs. Nothing went on in the neighborhood that the spirited widow didn't know about.

Jill returned her attention to the house. She squinted at the upstairs windows, looking for a sign that anyone was home, and was only mildly pleased to see nothing but darkness. Although that was good news, the bad news was that along with her letter, she'd left her key to the house.

Slowly trudging from the sidewalk to the circular driveway, her mind scrambled for the best solution. She definitely didn't want Spenser to see that letter if she could help it, which meant breaking into the house. When she got close to the front porch, she tilted her head back and frowned at the second story.

If there was the slimmest chance of an unlocked window it would belong to one of the rooms up there. But even that was pushing it. Spenser was far too attentive to overlook something like that.

Her gaze rose higher. The chimney stood out in the moonlight.

Nah. That would be stupid.

Of course, she wasn't wearing all that Santa padding and it hadn't been *that* tight a squeeze the last time. She briskly shook her head, amazed at her own foolishness, and took another step toward the porch steps.

She stopped again and cast another speculative look at

the roof. Of course, wiggling down a chimney seemed like a small price to pay for someone you loved.

The unsettling idea took a minute to process and sink in. But there was no mistake. She loved Spenser.

Not wanting to waste another second, she hurried toward the stairs, not quite sure what she was going to do next. The sudden screech of tires made her spin toward the street.

A dark sedan was silently parked where the taxi had been. Behind it, a familiar silver Mercedes careened to a halt. Maury climbed out from the driver's side at the same time two hulking figures exited the sedan. She recognized them immediately as the two who'd followed her to the mall.

Jill's pulse skidded out of control but she told herself not to panic. This was Maury. She could handle this. Her gaze skidded toward the goons leaning against their car.

Or she could scream her lungs out and hope Mrs. Peyton was near the window.

"Where's the money, Jill?" Maury asked in a voice that sounded alien and threatening. He didn't hurry, but strutted confidently toward her.

His question startled her. "What money?"

"Going back to the apartment was really stupid, Jill. I'm surprised at you. Don't be stupid anymore. Give me the cash."

"I honestly don't know what you're talking about."

"Come on, Jill. Let's do this the easy way." He wore a dark suit, dark shirt, his black hair slicked back. When he smiled suddenly, it gave her the creeps.

"Maury, I swear I don't know anything about any money. Are you talking about the deposit?"

"That I already got back. I want the six hundred and forty dollars."

She'd taken a couple of steps back, but stopped as her

heel hit the first stair, a surge of relief making her a little light-headed. She laughed. "I signed over my check to the agency and included that in the deposit. You didn't think I just took it, did you?" That sudden thought made her sick. She was no thief.

"I want the damn money, Jill," he said, moving closer.

In the distance, a siren wailed. The goons pushed away from the car. A cloud briefly shadowed the moon.

She stumbled back. "Maury, you don't understand—"

"Do you have the money?" His tone was harsh.

Behind her, light suddenly flooded the porch.

The siren pressed closer, red and yellow lights flashing at the end of the street.

"What's going on out here?" Spenser's voice boomed from the doorway. "Jill? Are you okay?"

Relief swamped her as she turned to see him move onto the porch. She couldn't see his face. The light receded behind him. And she wasn't sure she wanted to. He'd have read her note.

"Jill? Give me the money if you don't want trouble." Maury's voice was close. Startled, she swung around toward him. If he said anything else, she couldn't hear him. Ear-splitting noise shattered the peaceful night as a fire truck screamed to a halt in front of them.

Maury pivoted toward the truck, anger and fear distorting his features. The two henchmen looked at each other, then at Maury, straightening as if ready to bolt.

Two firemen leaped from the truck. Maury sprang toward Jill and grabbed her purse. Startled, she was too late with the swing she took at him, and ended up spinning around into Spenser's arms.

"Jill, stay here," Spenser ordered, looking her directly in the face, his hands gripping her upper arms. "Will you do that?"

Her eyes widened in disbelief. "He took my purse."

"Dammit, Jill."

"Where's the fire?" the first fireman shouted as his large booted feet ate up the ground between them.

"Not here," Spenser said, frowning.

"Stop that guy," Jill yelled, twisting in the direction of Maury's retreating form and trying to squirm away from Spenser.

"She's on the roof again."

A loud shrill feminine voice bellowed from across the yard. Jill quit struggling and everyone turned toward Mrs. Peyton. The elderly bleach-blond woman waddled across the grass between the two houses. As soon as she saw Jill, she made an abrupt stop, her hand clutching the lapels of her blue-plaid flannel robe.

"I thought you were on the roof," she said, looking nervously from Jill to the firemen to Spenser. "She was eyeing the chimney again," she added lamely, her shoulders sagging.

"Did you call this in?" the fireman asked the woman, pushing back his massive helmet with an irritated jerk.

"She got stuck the last time," Mrs. Peyton said hotly, her voice rising in self-defense.

A short spurt of siren blasted the night, and everyone turned toward the street. A police cruiser pulled up beside the fire truck, directly behind the silver Mercedes. Maury was just climbing in, yelling at his two associates to get out of his way. The dark sedan pulled sharply away from the curb, fishtailed and rammed the fire truck.

"Would somebody stop that guy," Jill hollered. She broke away from Spenser and sprinted down the driveway toward the Mercedes.

He lit after her as the two policemen rushed out of their car to check out the banged-up sedan.

"Not them," Jill yelled. "Get the other guy."

She didn't have to worry. Maury was hemmed in between two vehicles. There was nowhere for him to go. Except on foot. Out of breath, she slid to a stop at the driver's door, Spenser nearly colliding with her.

Maury jerked open the door, almost slamming it into her midsection. He flung the purse at her. "Remember, I tried to help you," he said in an overly loud voice. "Now, all I can offer is a good lawyer."

"Help me?" Snagging the pocketbook, she glared at him. "Why would I need a lawyer?"

"May I?" Spenser asked, although it clearly wasn't a question. He took the purse from her and after quickly finding her wallet, leafed through a stack of crisp brand-new currency. His gaze raised to pierce Maury with a feral look. "Hot off the press, huh?"

"I don't know anything about that," Maury said, adjusting his monogrammed cuffs. Throughout a brief silence, he returned Spenser's steely gaze. "I'm not saying another word until I talk to my lawyer."

TWO HOURS LATER, Jill sat in the family room, wrapped in an afghan, staring at the Christmas tree, a cup of hot chocolate growing cold on the table beside her. When she heard Spenser enter the room, she huddled deeper into the comforting wool and slowly forced herself to look at him.

They had a lot to say to each other. So much had happened in the last couple of hours; she had no idea what he was thinking of her at the moment. At least she knew he didn't think her guilty of being in cahoots with Maury and his counterfeit ring. After all, she was the one who'd mistakenly deposited the phony money that had been earmarked for the Caribbean black market.

She was also the reason why Maury was in custody right now.

"Did Mindy go back to sleep?" she asked.

"A few minutes ago."

"I'm sorry I ruined Christmas Eve for her."

"Are you kidding? All the commotion gave her an opportunity to be looking out for Santa."

Jill smiled, even though Spenser didn't. He sat across from her, a myriad of questions in his darkened eyes. As much as she wanted to look away, she squarely met his gaze. He was waiting for her to make the first move.

She took a deep breath and allowed herself a moment to get composed. Because for the first time in her life, she wasn't going to run away. As tough as it was to stay and face the consequences, right now, it would be tougher for her to leave.

"I owe you an apology," she said, gathering the afghan more securely around her. "I shouldn't have left like I did."

"No," he agreed, and leaned back in his chair, something flickering in his eyes that gave her hope. "Why did you come back?"

"I forgot to decorate my tree," she said, and immediately regretted the flip remark. A sad smile crossed her face. Flip wasn't going to cut it.

She had to tell him the truth and accept whatever consequences resulted. Maybe he'd tell her to go to hell.

Sudden alarm started her heart pounding. She wouldn't blame him if he told her to get out. After all, what did she have to offer? And then another thought struck. Maybe he simply didn't care. That would hurt the most. "You don't seem too upset."

His gaze roamed her face. She tried not to let the panic

show. She was going to do it...tell him she loved him no matter what he said or thought of her.

"I wasn't upset." He shrugged, and her heart thudded. "I would have found you."

"Found me?"

He locked his eyes on hers and said nothing.

He hadn't given up on her. Her father had. But not Spenser. She squinted at him. "You would have looked for me?" she asked, hope and joy blossoming like a new spring rose.

"Yes," he said without hesitation.

"Oh, Spenser." His simple admission told her more than anything else could. She leaped off the chair and flung herself at him. Laughing, he toppled on his side and she followed him down, stretching out beside him, kissing his face, his jaw, his neck.

"Jill?" His laughter ended in a moan, and in a hoarse voice, he said, "Tell me why you came back."

She pulled slightly away to look at him, her insides twisting and cramping. Words she'd never spoken before teetered precariously on her tongue.

"Because I love you," she said, and swallowed. "And no matter what happened when I finally faced Maury, it couldn't be worse than never seeing you again." She held her breath. She hadn't stumbled over the words the way she thought she might. And he didn't look as though he wanted to jump off the roof. Maybe she was going to live through this, after all.

He lifted a hand to touch her hair. "I love you," he said, his eyes meeting hers. "I'm not an impulsive person," he added, and smiled when she did. "And I know this seems sudden, but I have never felt about anyone the way I feel about you."

Her breath caught, and before she could say anything, he

added, "But you've got to promise me you'll lose the Santa suit."

She laughed and cried at the same time, kissing his cheek, his nose, his lips. "I promise," she whispered.

"And one more thing?"

She gazed at him through watery eyes.

"Say you'll marry me." He looked vulnerable suddenly, and Jill didn't think she could possibly love him any more than she did at that moment.

Sniffing, she grabbed his lapels and pulled him toward her. "Listen, buddy," she said. "Just try and get rid of me."

She'd taken him by surprise and they rolled off the couch onto the floor, laughing, kissing, until they heard the soft echo of sleigh bells coming from the chimney.

Jill stared wide-eyed at the fireplace.

Spenser smiled, hugging her to him. "Sometimes you just have to believe."

Epilogue

JILL STEERED Mindy through the busy mall, around the throng of holiday shoppers and toward Santa's sleigh throne. When they approached the department store where everything had started last year, Jill slowed down, smiling at the display window.

Mindy glanced up at her. "We have to hurry. After I give Santa my list, Daddy wants to meet us for ice cream."

"Okay, sweetie." Jill nodded absently, letting Mindy pull her past the store. She wondered where Spenser had sneaked off to. She knew for a fact that he'd already bought all her Christmas gifts. No matter how well he'd hidden them, she'd already found each and every one. She shook her head. After a year of marriage, you'd think he'd quit underestimating her.

"The line isn't that long," Mindy said as they neared Santa.

Relief eased the tension in Jill's cramped shoulders. She'd thought they might be in for a long haul, had even suspected that was why Spenser had pulled his disappearing act. Although she had not a single reason to think that. He was a devoted father, and he never expected Jill to do anything he wouldn't do himself.

In fact, it had taken months for Jill to coax him into flying again. Sometimes, she selfishly wished she hadn't. Although he refused to take on more than an overnight assignment, she missed him horribly when he was away.

Jill sighed. She hated feeling so emotional these days, so out of sorts. But there had been so many changes in her life. Such wonderful changes that sometimes she had to pinch herself to believe it all. For the first time in her life, she felt loved.

Yet things were about to change again. And the thought of talking to Spenser returned the tension to her shoulders.

She and Mindy immediately stationed themselves in line and within minutes, they were next up. Santa beckoned Mindy toward him, and she promptly tugged at Jill's hand.

Laughing, Jill tried to disengage herself. "I know you're not afraid to go up there by yourself."

"Come on, Mom," Mindy insisted with an extra tug, and Jill stumbled forward, stunned.

Although she and Mindy got along incredibly well, the girl had never called her "Mom" before. Swallowing hard, Jill dabbed at the flour smudged near Mindy's ear from their cookie-baking marathon earlier. Which made Jill think of the Spenser cookbook with her name in it, and she blinked and swallowed all over again.

"Okay," she whispered, and allowed Mindy to pull her along.

"Ho-ho-ho." Santa patted his lap. "Two for the price of one. This is my lucky day."

Jill squinted at the man as she urged Mindy in his direction. There was something familiar about him.

"There's room for both of you," he said, and after sitting Mindy on one thigh, he patted the other one.

"Spenser?" Jill whispered, her eyes widening.

Mindy giggled, and darting a glance toward the line, she cupped her mouth. "Shh, Mom, you'll ruin it for the kids."

Behind wire-rimmed spectacles, Spenser's hazel gaze shot to his daughter. Slowly, it swung toward Jill, and the corners of his eyes crinkled. "Have you both been very good girls?"

"The best," Mindy said, grinning, displaying a gap from a lost tooth. Then she whispered too loud, "Give her the present."

Spenser shook his head, laughing, then reached behind and produced a small box wrapped in red foil and a large gold bow.

Mindy's eyes rounded. "Does she get to open it now?"

"Yes, but only because it's not really a Christmas gift."

Jill stared at the box for a second, then tore into it. There was lots of tissue paper, but as she pushed it aside, she saw the booties. One pink pair. One blue pair.

She looked up in amazement. "How did you know?"

Mindy stuck her hand in the box and rifled through the tissue. "That's it?" She frowned. "That's a dumb present."

"How did you know?" Jill asked again, and Spenser's lips curved beneath the bushy fake beard, making her heart soar. She'd been afraid to tell him. Now she knew how foolish that fear was.

"Would I underestimate your ability for the unexpected?" Spenser chuckled. "The only thing I don't know is which variety," he said above Mindy's confused stare. "Now, would you put me out of my misery and tell me if we'll be needing pink or blue?"

Jill smiled. "Right on both counts."

His phony white eyebrows drew together. "What?"

"Do twins run in your family?" Jill asked, laughing, happy that he'd underestimated her, after all.

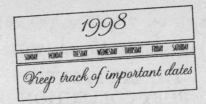

1998

SUNDAY MONDAY TUESDAY WEDNESDAY THURSDAY FRIDAY SATURDAY

Keep track of important dates

Three beautiful and colorful calendars that celebrate some of the most popular trends in America today.

Look for:

Just Babies—a 16 month calendar that features a full year of absolutely adorable babies!

1998 CALENDAR
Just Babies
16 months of adorable bundles of joy!

Hometown Quilts
1998 Calendar
A 16 month quilting extravaganza!

Hometown Quilts—a 16 month calendar featuring quilted art squares, plus a short history on twelve different quilt patterns.

Inspirations—a 16 month calendar with inspiring pictures and quotations.

Inspirations

A 16 month calendar that will lift your spirits and gladden your heart

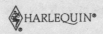

Steeple Hill™

HARLEQUIN®

Value priced at $9.99 U.S./$11.99 CAN., these calendars make a perfect gift!

Available in retail outlets in August 1997.   CAL98

Coming in August 1997!

THE BETTY NEELS RUBY COLLECTION

August 1997—Stars Through the Mist
September 1997—The Doubtful Marriage
October 1997—The End of the Rainbow
November 1997—Three for a Wedding
December 1997—Roses for Christmas
January 1998—The Hasty Marriage

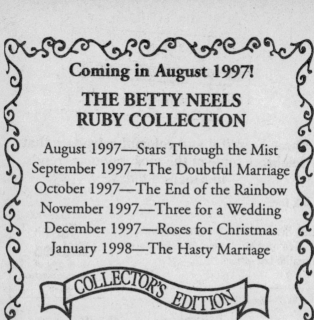

COLLECTOR'S EDITION

This August start assembling the
Betty Neels Ruby Collection. Six of the
most requested and best-loved titles have
been especially chosen for this collection.
From August 1997 until January 1998,
one title per month will be available to avid
fans. Spot the collection by the lush ruby red
cover with the gold Collector's Edition banner
and your favorite author's name—Betty Neels!

Available in August at your favorite retail outlet.

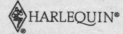

HARLEQUIN®

LOVE & LAUGHTER™

Jo Montgomery had her life planned out—a satisfying career, marriage with longtime boyfriend Alan Parish and definitely *NO KIDS!* Then she met gorgeous widower—and father—John Sterling. And Jo found out the hard way that:

Kids
Is a 4-Letter Word

(#35)–January 1998

For Alan Parish, being left at the altar was a blessing. Thank God he was still single! And since the honeymoon was paid for, what was wrong with inviting his friend Pam to enjoy it with him? But when the fictional honeymoon became fact, Alan discovered that:

Wife
Is a 4-Letter Word

(#37)–February 1998

Be sure to watch for these two hilarious romances by talented newcomer
Stephanie Bond

Available in January 1998
wherever Harlequin books are sold.

The romance continues in four spin-off books.

Discover what destiny has in store when Lina, Arianna, Briana and Molly crack open their fortune cookies!

PAIN CAN BE THE MIDWIFE OF JOY

THIS CHILD IS MINE
Janice Kaiser
Superromance #761
October 1997

NEVER JUDGE A BOOK BY ITS COVER

DOUBLE TAKE
Janice Kaiser
Temptation #659
November 1997

DISCOVER YOUR DREAMS AND DISCOVER YOURSELF

THE DREAM WEDDING
M.J. Rodgers
Intrigue #445
December 1997

FOLLOW YOUR DREAM

JOE'S GIRL
Margaret St. George
American Romance #710
January 1998

Available wherever Harlequin books are sold.

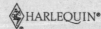
HARLEQUIN®

Look us up on-line at: http://www.romance.net

FCSPIN

Every month there's another title from one
of your favorite authors!

October 1997
Romeo in the Rain by Kasey Michaels
When Courtney Blackmun's daughter brought home Mr. Tall,
Dark and Handsome, Courtney wanted to send the young
matchmaker to her room! Of course, that meant the single
New Jersey mom would be left alone with the irresistibly
attractive Adam Richardson....

November 1997
Intrusive Man by Lass Small
Indiana's Hannah Calhoun had enough on her hands taking
care of her young son, and the last thing she needed was a
man complicating things—especially Max Simmons, the
gorgeous cop who had eased himself right into her little boy's
heart…and was making his way into hers.

December 1997
Crazy Like a Fox by Anne Stuart
Moving in with her deceased husband's—*eccentric*—family
in Louisiana meant a whole new life for Margaret Jaffrey and
her nine-year-old daughter. But the beautiful young widow
soon finds herself seduced by the slower pace and the much-
too-attractive cousin-in-law, Peter Andrew Jaffrey....

**BORN IN THE USA: Love, marriage—
and the pursuit of family!**

Available at your favorite retail outlet!